Pastors and Masters

Pastors and Masters

Ivy Compton-Burnett

ET REMOTISSIMA PROPE

Modern Voices

Modern Voices
Published by Hesperus Press Limited
4 Rickett Street, London SW6 1RU
www.hesperuspress.com

Pastors and Masters © Estate of Ivy Compton-Burnett, 1925
First published by Hesperus Press Limited, 2009

Foreword © Sue Townsend, 2009

Designed and typeset by Fraser Muggeridge studio
Printed in Jordan by Al-Khayyam Printing Press

ISBN: 978-1-84391-453-2

Contents

Foreword

Scratch below the skin of any person and a little blood will ooze, but scratch below the skin of most writers and the blood will gush, and the wound will never, properly, heal.

It is astonishing how many writers have suffered a significant bereavement: the loss of a parent or sibling in their childhood. Faced with such overwhelming hurt, it is common for such wounded children to construct a carapace around themselves, in an attempt to avoid feeling more pain.

Ivy Compton-Burnett was such a child. She was the first born of James, a homeopathic doctor, and Kathleen, who was beautiful but neurotic. It was her father's second marriage and he brought with him five young children. In 1901, when Ivy was sixteen, her father died leaving a total of twelve children. Her mother went into deep mourning. For over a year she insisted that the children, including the baby, wore black.

Ivy's mother grew increasingly despotic and used self-pity as a weapon and ran her household as though she were the leader of a totalitarian regime. She died in 1911. Then Guy, Ivy's favourite brother and soul mate, died of pneumonia. Another favourite brother was killed on the Somme and her two youngest sisters swallowed poison and died in their bedroom on Christmas Day.

In view of these grotesque misfortunes one can only think that Ivy's carapace was, by now, almost complete. However, she never referred to her childhood and wrote on the jacket of her old Penguin editions:

I have had such an uneventful life that there is little information to give. I was educated with my brothers in the country as a child, and later went on to Holloway College, and took a degree in Classics. I lived with my family when I was quite young but for most of my life have had my own flat in London. I see a good deal of good many friends, not all of them writing people. And there is really no more to say.

What she learned from her childhood was that death snatched love away and that nothing was ever as it seemed on the surface, that everything was sub-text. It is perhaps significant that none of the twelve children in the Compton-Burnett household had children themselves and that none of the eight girls ever married, and it is no surprise that Ivy, given her love of books and formidable intelligence, became a writer.

Pastors and Masters is her second novel. Her first, *Dolores*, was published in 1911, the year her mother died. Later in life Ivy did not acknowledge its publication, preferring to forget this early work.

Pastors and Masters caused a stir in English literary circles. *The New Statesman* wrote, 'It is astonishing, amazing. It is like nothing else in the world. It is work of genius.'

The story takes place in an old university town in a private day-school for boys between the ages of ten and fourteen. The owner and headmaster, seventy-year-old Nicholas Herrick, spends only ten minutes a day at the school when he takes morning prayers. He wastes most of his day lazing in his study, supposedly working on his novel, which he hopes will impress the world and compensate somehow for his lack of a degree. His unmarried sister, Emily Herrick, is also unqualified to teach and concerns herself with the cheese-paring domestic arrangements. The school is actually run, albeit badly, by Charles Merry, a fifty-year-old man who has no vocation for teaching, and no degree, but is in need of his small salary as he has to support four young daughters. Mrs Merry also has no teaching qualifications but this does not prevent her from doing so. The only person on the teaching staff with a degree is young

Mr Burgess, who scraped through the final part of his degree whilst working at the school. These inadequate adults keep the boys in a permanent state of anxiety: by issuing instructions and then immediately countermanding them, addressing them with withering sarcasm, by talking about them as though they were not in the room, and were merely ciphers. Most of the boys are not characterised, though there is an unfortunate child called Johnson, who seems to be the scapegoat of the school. One can imagine that poor Johnson cries himself to sleep at night, dreading the next morning when he must return to school.

This short novel is written almost entirely in dialogue. My eighteen-year-old granddaughter read it aloud to me because I have been registered blind for six years and cannot read without huge, illuminated and magnified devices, which turns the reading process into a long and tedious haul. But hearing it spoken gives one the immediate impression that the characters in *Pastors and Masters* use language as soldiers use their weapons, to injure and kill. Few of the more commendable human qualities are to be found in these pages. Human interaction consists of a series of skirmishes and fatal hits. There is little human kindness. The overall impression is of a bleak claustrophobic world, populated by people desperately trying to suck oxygen from an arid and stultifying atmosphere.

Thankfully, Ms Compton-Burnett's black humour saves the reader from lapsing into morbid introspection. But she herself once said, 'My books are hard not to put down,' so the reader will not find this book to be an easy read, some concentration is needed until one becomes familiar with the rhythm and tone of Ms Compton-Burnett's sentences and then there are glorious passages ahead.

A few months before I was asked to write this foreword I came across a photograph of Ivy Compton-Burnett of Cecil Beaton's work. A strong, guarded face stared back at me. She was holding a cigarette as though it were a permanent extension of her fingers. I knew nothing about her at the time, apart from the fact that she was a high priestess of English literature and that Virginia Woolf lost sleep at night from worrying about their rivalry. Mrs Woolf may have worried less had she known that deep inside Ms Compton-Burnett's indomitable black-clad figure was a wounded child longing for love and recognition.

– Sue Townsend, 2009

Pastors and Masters

I

'Well, this is a nice thing! A nice thing this school-mastering! Up at seven, and in a room with a black fire… I should have thought it might have occurred to one out of forty boys to poke it… and hard at work, before other men think it time to be awake! And while you are about it, don't pile on as much coal as it would take the day's profits of the school to pay for. And here is a thing I have to see every morning of my life! Here is a thing I have to be degraded by, every morning when I come down to an honest day's work, a middle-aged man working to support his family! I am surprised to see people with such a want of self-respect. I admit that I am. I would rather see a boy come in roundly late, than slip in on the stroke, half dressed and half asleep, and pass as being in time. It is an ungentlemanly thing to do.'

Mr Merry, a tall, thin man about fifty, leaned back in his chair, and fixed on his pupils his little, pale, screwed up eyes, to which he had the gift of imparting an alluring kindness. His feelings towards them, affection, disgust, pride and despair, seemed to oust each other over his face.

'Yes, I am sick and tired of this sort of thing. I will not mince matters with you. And get to your seats without upsetting everything on your way, will you please? Oh, who would be a school-master? I should not be doing my duty to you all, if I did not warn you all against it. And I suppose it is a good thing to have the east wind from an east window blowing in upon forty people, thirty-nine of them growing boys, before their breakfast on a March morning? And… one, two, three, four, five, six, seven… it takes eleven boys to shut a window, does it? And I suppose I cannot make a few remarks, without having you all fidgeting and gaping and behaving like a set of clodhoppers instead of gentlemen? Get to your work at once, and don't look up again before the gong.'

Mr Merry gave a gesture of despairing acquiescence as the boys obeyed this summons without his endorsing it. He followed them down to their basement dining room.

Mrs Merry, a smooth-headed, mild-looking woman with a grieved expression, was standing at the head of a long table, pouring out tea. Her four little girls were seated near her. A thin dark lady of forty, matron and teacher of music and French, was cutting bread.

'Well, Mother,' said Mr Merry, in the tone of a tender husband and tried man.

'Well, dear,' said Mrs Merry, without raising her eyes.

'Good morning, Miss Basden,' said Mr Merry, with the almost exaggerated courtesy due to a lady he employed.

'Good morning, Mr Merry,' said Miss Basden, in a tone in which equality, respect and absorption in her duty were rather remarkably mingled.

'Now, look here,' said Mr Merry, 'I have never had such an ungentlemanly set of boys. Now, go out again, all of you, and come in like gentlemen meeting a lady for the first time in the day.'

A retirement from the room was succeeded by a chorus of 'Good morning, Mrs Merry'.

'Good morning, boys,' said Mrs Merry.

'Have you all met Miss Basden already today?' Mr Merry inquired, looking round frigidly.

'Good morning, Miss Basden.'

'Good morning, boys,' said Miss Basden, in a casual tone, still cutting.

'Hillman!' said Mr Merry, 'How often am I to say that I will not have sitting down before grace is said? Pray do not show your nature to the rest of us.'

Hillman gained his feet.

'For these and all other mercies may we be given thankful hearts,' said Mr Merry, his eyes taking a covert general survey.

'Johnson, I am disgusted! I am more. I cannot tell you before ladies what I think of you. I hoped I should never have a boy in my school who would not control himself for a moment to give his attention to sacred things. What was it, pray, that you had to say, of such importance that it could not wait for a second?'

Johnson, who had been observing that it was wise to ask for thankful hearts for such mercies, was silent.

'Now,' said Mr Merry, preparing again to bend his head, 'we will say grace again, and I hope nothing so humiliating will occur a second time. I shall not speak of the matter, Johnson.'

Mrs Merry and Miss Basden bowed their heads a little lower than before, though it was hardly to be thought that their experience had not been suitable.

'I cannot bear to see a sulky boy,' said Mr Merry, throwing a disgusted glance at Johnson.

'Will you have tea or coffee, dear?' said Mrs Merry.

'Oh, either, either, anything will do for me.'

'I always arrange for you to have your choice, dear.'

'Yes, Mother, yes. You take good care of me. You spend your life taking care of people, I'm afraid.' Mr Merry looked round on the boys with an air of rebuking ingratitude.

'Yes, I have done a good deal of taking care in my time. I think I have done very little else.'

'Well, Mrs Merry, we must begin to take care of you,' said Miss Basden, putting the toastrack near to Mrs Merry.

'How did you sleep, Miss Basden?' said Mr Merry, in an extremely interested manner.

'Mrs Merry,' Miss Basden said, in a rather high monotone, 'the boys are saying that the marmalade is watery. I am telling them that no water is used in marmalade, that marmalade does not contain water, so I do not see how it can be.'

'I do not see how it can be, either, but of course I wish to be told if anything is not as nice as it can be. Let me taste the marmalade.'

Miss Basden offered a spoon from the pot.

'It seems to me that it is very nice. Perhaps I am not a judge of marmalade. I do not care to eat it on bread with butter myself. One or the other is enough for me. But it seems to me to be very nice.'

'Mother, don't water the boys' preserves,' said Mr Merry, nodding his head up and down. 'Don't try to make things go further than they will go, you know. The game isn't worth the candle.'

'I do not understand you, dear. There is never any extra water in preserves. They would not keep if they had water in them. There would not be any object in it. It would be less economical, not more.'

'Oh well, Mother, I don't know anything about the kitchen business and that. But if the marmalade is not right, let us have it right another time. That is all I mean.'

'I do not think you know what you mean, dear.'

'No, Mother, no, very likely I don't.'

'The housekeeping is not your province, Mr Merry,' said Miss Basden. 'You will have us coming and telling you how to teach Latin, if you are not careful.'

'Ah, Miss Basden, ah, you saucy lady! Not such a babel down at that part of the room! Not such a babel. Do you hear me? Be quiet, or go away, and leave the room to civilised people.' Mr Merry looked fiercely towards the other end of the table, which certainly tended to be the noisier.

'Mr Burgess is not going to allow us much of his company at breakfast this morning,' said Miss Basden.

'I wonder if Fanny called him,' said Mrs Merry.

'Yes, she called him,' said Miss Basden.

'Ah! He's fond of the sheets, is Mr Burgess. He is fond of the sheets,' said Mr Merry, while the boys found this talk of the undermaster a cause for nudges and smiles.

'I never can understand how people can lie in bed in daylight,' said Miss Basden.

'Now it would do you good to do a little more of it, Miss Basden,' said Mr Merry. 'You do too much of the other thing, as I always tell you. It would do you good to do a little more of it.'

'Oh, that sort of advice does not have much effect on me, Mr Merry,' said Miss Basden, again cutting bread.

'You give poor Miss Basden a great deal of work to do,' said Mr Merry, looking down the rows of boys with vague disapproval.

'You must make haste, all of you. Mr Herrick will be here to read prayers in a minute,' said Mrs Merry.

'Mother, ought not Mr Burgess' bacon to be kept hot?' said Mr Merry, his voice conveying criticism of Mr Burgess, and the need of diplomacy with him.

'We do not usually expect people to come down when breakfast is over,' said Mrs Merry. 'The bacon was hot when it was brought in.'

'Fanny,' said Mr Merry, in a tone of apology to the maid who was waiting, 'just put Mr Burgess' bacon down in the fender, will you? Thank you Fanny, thank you very much.'

'I do not like more bread cut than will be eaten,' said Mrs Merry.

'Mrs Merry, several boys asked for some more only a minute ago,' said Miss Basden.

'If you asked for it, eat it,' said Mr Merry. 'If you asked for it, eat it. Do not give the trouble of cutting it, and then cause more disturbance by refusing it. If you have eaten all the rest, you can easily manage a little more.'

As the chairs were pushed from the table, Mr Herrick entered. He was the actual owner of the school, Mr Merry being his partner. He was a short, impressive old man with a solid neck and head, heavy grey hair, and features with a touch of the Jew.

He was a writer, and kept his time for his own, and read prayers to the school by way of acting as its head. He had placed the school in the old university town, to be near the college where he had spent his youth. Mr Merry stood out in the room, half bowing towards him.

'Good morning, Mr Herrick, good morning. It is a frosty day. That is why we are a little late. Frost makes good appetites, that is one good thing that it does. We were just going to get up from the table, when there was a demand for more bread and butter. By no means the first demand, eh, boys?'

The boys signified amongst themselves their sense of the doubleness of Mr Merry's nature. Mr Herrick half bowed in his turn to Mr Merry, quite bowed to Mrs Merry, and again to Miss Basden, nodded to the boys, sat down and opened the Bible. As he did so, there appeared Mr Burgess, who walked into the room with an air of being unconscious that he would not find things at a natural stage for a newcomer.

'Ah, Mr Burgess,' said Mr Merry, as Mr Burgess' eyes began to take in that matters had gone so far, 'we have been talking about you. The only thing we could do, as we could not talk to you. There is a place that is very comfortable on a frosty morning. Eh?'

Mr Merry's way of addressing his head and his junior for the ears of the boys had grown into a habit.

'Am I late?' said Mr Burgess, in a casual, courteous tone.

'Good morning, Burgess,' said Herrick, his eyes on his book.

Mr Merry sat down.

Mr Burgess, as just perceiving that prayers were about to be held, took his seat.

'Pray do not allow us to keep you waiting for breakfast, Burgess,' said Herrick. 'Take your seat at the table, I beg of you.'

'Oh no, Mr Herrick. I shall like to… take my part with you as usual, thank you. It matters very little to me what time

I breakfast. Often I am out of doors for an hour or two before. I have very little sense of time in the morning.'

There was a titter from the boys.

'Yes, Mr Herrick,' said Mr Merry, with an air of apology, and a fierce sidelong glance, 'he goes out sometimes before breakfast to get his exercise, you know. Young fellows always will be thinking of keeping fit, you know.'

'Mr Burgess will have to take out the boys this morning, Mr Merry,' said Miss Basden, leaning forward.

Mr Burgess sat with an air exclusively expectant of Herrick's reading. He greatly disliked Miss Basden, though there was a belief among the boys that he designed to wed her. Herrick began to read, and Miss Basden listened with colour deepened, and Mr Burgess with an appearance of keen interest. When the assembly rose from its knees, Herrick at once bore the Bible from the room. Mr Burgess stepped to the window, and sought the signs of the sky.

'Come now, Mr Burgess,' said Mr Merry, making amends to his junior by lifting his bacon himself from the fender. 'If you are not hungry by this time, you should be. Pray do not hurry. The boys will not hurt by a little waiting.'

'Oh, thank you, Mr Merry,' said Mr Burgess, coming to the table, and taking up the sugar tongs. 'I had no idea of the time. But boys do not hurt by a little waiting, that is true. Adams, just see if my paper is in the hall.'

Adams obeyed with a feeling of respect for Mr Burgess, which Mr Merry was almost disposed to share. Mr Burgess received his paper, and put down his fork to turn its pages. Mr Merry inquired if the boys were waiting for their footman to bring them their boots.

Mr Burgess, left to himself, set to his breakfast with an energy he had not shown that day, except at his toilet. Even if boys did hurt by waiting, these would not have suffered. He put his paper in his pocket, and at a distance from the house began to read. Returning, he saw Mr Merry at a window. He looked back at the paper, and in a moment turned to the boy and said: 'So you see, Parliament thought that Bill a wrong one, and it was thrown out.'

'Well, what news, Mr Burgess?' said Mr Merry, coming into the hall.

'Oh, nothing to speak of. Just a few little things to glance at,' said Mr Burgess, defining the scope of his attention. 'Would you care to have the paper, Mr Merry?'

'Thank you, Mr Burgess, thank you. I am a poor man. I don't rise to *The Times*.'

Mr Burgess went without a word to the classroom where the elder pupils were taught. Mr Merry shuffled into the other, and sat down before the younger boys. He had not been prompted to the teacher's life by his liberal education. There were other and more urgent reasons for his choice.

Mrs Merry taught the scripture of the school, and there was a general sense of her fitness for the task, based upon her temperament rather than her scholarship. Mr Merry often mentioned the fact of her teaching it to parents.

The boys, who had a tendency to giggle this morning, took their seats about her table.

'It is the scripture lesson,' she said, with peaceful lips. 'I think we are forgetting that.'

The boys read aloud a chapter verse by verse, and Mrs Merry added observations in a gentle, rather peculiar voice used only on these occasions. At questions she turned to the commentary, and read it out, and it was felt that difficulties had been met as far as reverence permitted. An especial discrepancy caused an increase of mirth. Mrs Merry looked straight at the questioner.

'I don't think we will cavil about it, Johnson. We will just think of it. That will be the best, and the most difficult thing. The book says nothing, you see.'

It was felt that a cheap effort had been made, but the laughter held its own.

Mrs Merry looked very long at a boy.

'It is only the Bible, Bentley, only the most sacred book in existence that you are laughing at.'

'It is only the Bible, Bentley.'

'I shall have to give you up, boys.'

Mrs Merry, with a look round that said many things, rose and walked from the room.

'Constant laughing and inattention make it impossible to teach them!'

Mr Merry entered, hunching his shoulders and driving his hands violently into his pockets.

'Well now, I am degraded. *I* am degraded. I feel it a personal humiliation to have to come and speak to people supposed to be gentlemen, about their making it impossible for a lady to teach them. For a lady to teach them holy things! There is an unspeakable thing to find happening in my school. I shall not speak of it. I cannot bring myself to do so. And I hope that no boy in this room will speak to me again today. Because I could not come down to his level, and there is the truth for him.'

It was Mrs Merry's birthday, and she knew that a present from the boys would be placed on the table at tea. It had been subscribed for by them in private consultation with Miss Basden, and chosen by that lady and Mrs Merry in the town together.

By teatime Mrs Merry had reached the state, which justified her yearly message, that she was prevented by a headache from appearing. The boys begged Miss Basden to approach her. Mr Merry sat vaguely ill at ease, kept as it were in bands by the parcel at the head of the table.

Mrs Merry sent word that she would try and come for a moment, and entered, flushed and unexpectant, and approached her place.

'Why, what is this? What can this be? Why, I do not understand this, boys.'

Miss Basden stepped forward and quickly cut the string, in
the manner of one tying gunpowder to a friend at the stake.

'Oh, boys,' said Mrs Merry. 'Oh, boys! Oh, what is this? Oh,
you should not spend your money on me. I had no expectation
of anything like this. And the very thing that I needed! Some
good fairy must have…'

Her voice failed.

'There, Mother, there you're not well,' said Mr Merry.
'You're not well, as you told us, Mother. And so you get upset.
We know how it is. It is just because you look after us all too
well. We know how pleased you are. So you need not trouble to
tell us any more. Come, have your tea, boys. Have your tea, and
it is very kind of you all. What is that commotion in the hall
above? Williams, just see what the commotion in the hall is.
Thank you, Williams, very much.'

It was reported that a lady was in the hall, and that Mr
Herrick requested that Mr Merry would join him.

'What a time to come to see a school! After keeping myself
free from seven in the morning, I am not allowed to have a cup
of tea in peace. People will be coming in the middle of the night
next. If there's a thing I can't bear, it's want of consideration.'

Mr Merry hastened up the stairs, and at the top caused his
face to undergo a change, preparatory to whatever final one
might be expedient.

'Oh, this is Mr Merry! What shame to call him away from his
boys! But I can only stay a moment so I shall not keep him.'

'Now, what a thing to be saying of me!' said Mr Merry,
taking the stranger's hand in both of his, with fond eyes. 'What
a thing to be saying of me! That I should think it a shame to be
called away to you. Not but what I am fond of my boys. Yes,
I am fond of my boys.'

'I saw such a dear little boy in the hall.'

'Ah, the little rascal! Little mischief that he is, always running about, when he ought to be at his books! Ah, well, they like a run from time to time. And he is not over strong, the little fellow. When he came to us, it went to my heart to see him. But my wife, she coddles him, you know. She coddles him, and he is a different boy.'

'Oh, how nice for an anxious mother to hear! Because we can't expect Mr Herrick to give his mind to all the little things a mother thinks of.'

'Oh, we won't tell Mr Herrick what we think of him,' said Mr Merry, as his chief followed his custom of leaving him unhampered play for his gifts. 'Perhaps he knows without our telling him. Sometimes I see him reading all about himself in the papers.'

'And about the general teaching of the school? Mr Herrick does not do a great deal of the ordinary work, does he?' Mr Merry reflected that Herrick had gone far in the minutes before his release. 'But of course you have masters to help you?'

'Now, I tell you a thing,' said Mr Merry, lifting his questioner's hand up and down, a picture of Mr Burgess before his eyes. 'You have confidence in us. In me and my wife, and my good helpers, and above all, in your boy. And there is one of us you won't be disappointed in. I can promise you that. And that is the last. And the first too, isn't he? Bless him, yes. And now there is a thing I want to say. I am here to make the boys happy. Little fellows away from home need to be made happy, you know. A master who is known all over the world is an enormous thing for a boy. I wish I had had as much in my younger days. But that is not quite all that is wanted. A mother knows that.'

On his way back through the hall, Mr Merry passed Mr Herrick without a word. The quality of Mr Merry's that gained him his bread was never alluded to between them.

'Well, there is another one come and gone, Mother. Another ship in the night. One never knows if anything will come of it. And a third of what comes out of one more boy won't overflow our coffers, will it?'

There was a titter from the boys.

'You get on with your tea,' said Mr Merry. 'And don't be so humiliatingly deceived as to think that another one of you would be of any advantage to anyone. Because such an idea would be humiliating to you. I can tell you that.'

'I do not think I could do with another boy,' said Mrs Merry, in a gentle, distinct tone.

'No, I should not like you to have anything more on you, Mrs Merry,' said Miss Basden.

'I don't know that I could either,' said Mr Burgess.

'Oh well, Mr Burgess, it wouldn't be too much on you,' said Mr Merry. 'We should like to see that. It would be all fitting in together for you, you know.'

Mr Burgess looked towards the window.

'I could always do with what had to be done with,' said Miss Basden. 'But the boys are quite mistaken, if they think that is any indication that they are needed by anyone. It is they who do the needing, I think.'

'Yes, Miss Basden,' said Mr Merry, nodding his head. 'It is indeed. They who do the needing! I should think so. I should be glad to be told of something they don't need. Because I don't know of anything, and that is the truth. I have just been hearing what is good enough for them. And I don't see anything about them that seems to call for it. I don't, indeed.'

2

'This is a good room to come back to,' said Herrick. 'That hall and the woman, and poor Merry shuffling up to do his duty! It made me shiver.'

'The sight of duty does make one shiver,' said Miss Herrick. 'The actual doing of it would kill one, I think.'

Emily Herrick was a tall, dark woman of fifty, half-sister to Herrick, with a face that somehow recalled an attractive idol's, iron-grey hair wound in plaits about her head, and a quick, deep voice.

'Merry knows what the duty is,' said Herrick. 'For my life, I don't.'

'One couldn't know what that duty was,' said Miss Herrick. 'It could only be felt, and perhaps you have too good a brain to do things in that way.'

'Let us leave it at that,' said Herrick.

'To think that you made the school!' said Emily. 'For it was you who made it. But of course you would do the creative part.'

'Yes, yes. And I could go on with it,' said Herrick.

'Of course you could,' said Emily. 'Woulddn't it be dreadful if you had to? Or if you did? It is almost dreadful that you could.'

'Yes, yes, it is,' said Herrick. 'I am an ordinary man.'

'I didn't mean that, darling,' said Emily. 'They say that teachers are born, not made. I know that schoolmasters are. And it was for a schoolmaster that we wanted Mr Merry.'

'It is for a schoolmaster we have him, anyhow,' said Herrick, sitting down at his desk.

'We must get out of the way of talking as if we were not honest, Nicholas,' said Emily. 'Anyone dishonest beside Mr Merry would be such a waste, and wastefulness in a school is so unwise. And Mr Merry has such charm in all that he does.'

'Merry is as open as the day,' said Herrick.

'Of course,' said Emily. 'That is what I meant. What charm could there be in dishonesty apart from that? Ought you to write any more today, dear? You have written more than usual, after being up all night.'

'I must go on separating my papers from old Crabbe's,' said Herrick. 'I found some things of his to go through, and I took some of my own to deal with. I knew it would be a long night. And he did not want much looking to, poor old Crabbe! Eighty-nine if he was a day, and a long sinking, as if he were not done out enough to die! He did not suffer, or hardly, and Masson and Bumpus and I watched by him at the end. Well, may we all do as well, die at ninety, easily, and with our friends round us. I had rather have friends than children. Men with the same outlook, not people looking for their main spell after we are gone! Well, Emily, I hope you will watch by me one day, as I watched by my old friend last night.'

'How beautifully you speak, darling!' said Emily, putting up her glass to look at her brother. 'And what a lot of good you have done! But I don't think you have made very kind plans for me. But perhaps you have left my deathbed to Mr Merry. There is no reason why he shouldn't take all your responsibilities. And to carry out your scheme for yourself for an outsider, is very rare of you. It could hardly be expected for one of your own family.'

'Ah, Emily,' said Herrick. 'You are twenty years younger than me. That is a thing we don't reckon with, but it is there. You don't look back or forward yet. We can't look forward really; but I think I can look back, and see my life as not lacking.'

Herrick lived in his disappointment that in letters he had done only critical work.

'I never look back on my life,' said Emily. 'It seems to be lacking in too much. You are so brave. There are William and Richard coming in. Guests must not be torn between admiration and anxiety, like people in the house.'

William Masson was a tall, large man in late middle-age, with loose limbs and loose clothes, and a weather-beaten, high-boned face. He seemed an example of all the uneasinesses combined into ease.

His companion was a little, dark man about fifty-six, with eyes sunk deeply in a working face.

The two were Fellows and dons at Herrick's college, and had meant romance for each other in youth. They had watched with Herrick at the deathbed of an old don, who had outlived his friends.

'Well, well,' said Herrick, 'so he is gone, the old man! We shall all be in his place one day. I have not to think of dying, surrounded by no one who is of my own kind and age. I can't help being glad that it is I who will have to look at you at the end, and not you to me.'

'He has been explaining to me,' said Emily, 'how I must die, unattended, while he has everybody kept alive for him. Nicholas has a wonderful gift for getting the best out of others. Think of Mr Merry.'

'I never cease to revere you for that, Herrick,' said Bumpus.

'I don't really revere Nicholas so much as Mr Merry,' said Emily. 'At least, I don't know. It was wonderful of Nicholas. I thought it mattered about Mr Merry's not being educated, as we were having him for a schoolmaster.'

'Yes, yes,' said Masson, in his high, stammering voice. 'I confess I rather thought that.'

'I did not think that,' said Bumpus. 'But I didn't know what did matter. The thing Merry has, isn't a thing one could guess.'

'Well, I always trust myself to judge a person at sight,' said Herrick. 'It is borne in upon me how a person is this or that. And I never find myself wrong. It is a gift that we are either with or without.'

'I believe gifts are like that,' said Bumpus.

'That is unkind, Dickie,' said Emily.

'You may have to see us all out, Herrick,' said Bumpus. 'You are past the danger age.'

'It is true that people who live to be seventy often do live to a great age,' said Herrick. 'They are in a sense out of danger.'

'I believe you seem to be planning my death,' said Emily, 'and without any arrangements at all for my deathbed. I hope you really do trust Mr Merry. Not only with the kind of trust that does for boys.'

'I am sixty,' said Masson. 'I claim also to be out of danger.'

'How exacting you all are about your amount of life!' said Bumpus. 'But of course we are all of us too good to die.'

'Well, well, we shall go on, doing things it has been in us to do here, that we have not done,' said Herrick. 'Ah, you do not think so, Emily. But this modern thought has you in its grip. You will grow out of it.'

'That will be nice and flexible of me, to grow out of things at fifty. They say that unusual people do develop very late.'

'I can't understand how people fear death,' said Herrick. 'It seems to me the most usual, natural thing, the last thing to be feared.'

'It is very usual. It might even be called universal,' said Bumpus.

'Don't be shallow and witty, Dickie,' said Emily. 'Nicholas was speaking of deeper truth.'

'I don't find anything shocking in seeing death ahead for me,' said Masson.

'No, you see it as it is, and yourself as you are,' said Bumpus. 'You are a long way above and below the rest of us. Below is the wrong word.'

'I should have thought he was above everything,' said Emily. 'I never like to think of it for him. It must be so hard to be like that. We are very brave to be able to talk about death. As brave as people who feel able to make their wills.'

'I always wondered why Crabbe never wrote,' said Herrick. 'He should have, shouldn't he? Shouldn't he not have written?'

'He never did. Not a line,' said Bumpus.

'I suppose a search after anything would be no good? I came across two or three scraps of different things. They are over there with my papers. But nothing of use.'

'No, no, no,' said Masson, firmly for him. 'A search for anything would be no good. He had nothing. He kept nothing. He was as light as air. He had no friends but ourselves. No contemporaries outliving him. There seems to be no one to be notified of his death.'

'That is how Nicholas wants me to be,' said Emily.

'Ah!' said Herrick.

'He has died as he lived,' went on Masson. 'Keeping nothing, needing nothing, asking nothing. A search of his rooms would be like searching a field.'

'You ought to write, William,' said Emily. 'You really have written, after saying things like that.'

'I have been thinking of writing again,' said Bumpus, putting his hand over his eyes. 'But I expect you all forget that I ever wrote. I don't know if you do remember how dramatic I was once as a youth, when – natural and reasonable it seemed to me then – I caused a manuscript to be put into the grave of a friend? I have written nothing since. I didn't mean that his death prevented me from writing later. That sort of thing comes out, if it is there. Though it is astonishing how many of us are capable of a single thing. But I have been writing a little book lately. I don't know why I should say little, except that it is short.'

'This is good to hear, Richard,' said Masson.

'Too good,' said Emily. 'I am so jealous for Nicholas. And he hasn't a story in his life, either. I mean, not a beautiful story.'

'I seem as if I must still write like a boy,' said Bumpus, more freely and eagerly. 'I find myself having to prune and tighten and mature. I don't know if it is breaking off in youth that makes me go on as if from where I left off. I don't believe we are ever much farther than at twenty-five.'

'I don't think I am,' said Herrick. 'For I also am thinking of bringing out a little book soon. Yes, Emily, you may look at me through that glass. I put off telling you until I should have the countenance of friends. For pleading guilty to turning real author at seventy! So we coincide, Bumpus. But I wish our ages coincided.'

'This is surely coincidence enough,' said Bumpus.

'I don't wish anything more,' said Emily. 'And how wonderful we are to have you coincide! It is selfless and beautiful of William and me.'

'That is what I feel,' said Bumpus.

'And I also am pleased with my little book,' went on Herrick, taking his sister's hand, 'and also don't know why I call it little, except that it is short. Short it is, and that's the truth, though I don't know why we should prefer a long book. If a book is a whole in itself, why is its length any matter?'

'But you do prefer a long one, darling,' said Emily. 'I always like that side of you. And now I know it is the simplicity of greatness. But don't make the book any longer. It is so careless of popular opinion to leave it short.'

'I wish… I wonder why we give voice to these wishes, but I wish old Crabbe had lived to see you with a book written, Herrick,' said Masson. 'He always said that you were a man who would write, if you put yourself to it.'

'Just what Nicholas has been saying of him,' said Emily. 'How beautiful they both are!'

'I have been a long fool, idle through seventy years of a good life,' said Herrick. 'But I don't know that I can wish that about Crabbe. I feel as if I should not have written this book, apart from his death, as if it would not have shaped itself in my mind as I now feel it. Of course there is no connection. None at all. None. But it came to me, as I sat there, the whole thing, the whole book. There it was. I can't explain it.'

'It doesn't seem good management,' said Emily. 'To keep your book to yourself for seventy years, and then have Mr Crabbe die to make it come out. But you are not a good manager, and Mr Merry can't do more than most of our life for both of us, and my death. And Mr Crabbe was ninety, and you had it all so nice for him.'

'How long will it take you to actually write it, Herrick?' said Bumpus.

'I have it this time,' said Herrick. 'I have been letting it grow in my head. Because of course in a way it has been there for some time. It is as good as written down. It was the form of it that flashed on me. I do things much in my head, as you know.'

'Oh, Nicholas, I didn't know. I do admire you,' said Emily.

'I think I have found myself at last,' said Herrick. 'I think that, God willing, I shall have done my little bit for my genera-tion, done what every man ought to do, before he dies.'

'You don't really think it is what every man ought to do,' said Emily. 'I do hope it isn't.'

'Assuming God, you wouldn't do much if he wasn't willing,' said Masson.

Bumpus laughed, and looked almost proudly at Masson.

'Are we going to be broad and wicked?' said Emily. 'I like that, because I am not very educated, and so still young in my mind. Really, it would be nice to have some religion, and not go on without ever any comfort. And I am not like Nicholas, who is really God's equal, and not his child at all. I think it is better not to have God than to be like that with him.'

'It is rather empty for him not to be had,' said Bumpus. 'He always seems to me a pathetic figure, friendless and childless and set up alone in a miserable way.'

'Yes, he has a touch of William in him,' said Emily. 'But you know he isn't childless. We give even our boys more advantages than that. Mrs Merry gives it to them.'

'You can have him childless in these days,' said Masson. 'Perhaps I do resemble him in that.'

'And he had such a personality,' said Emily. 'Such a superior, vindictive and over-indulgent one. He is one of the best drawn characters in fiction.'

'I really cannot listen to this,' said Herrick.

'Isn't it quietly conscientious of Herrick, to be behind the parents' backs what he is to their faces?' said Bumpus. 'What he would be to their face if he saw them.'

'I am deeply grateful to Merry,' said Herrick. 'Nobody knows what seeing them is.'

'Mr Merry does,' said Emily. 'I am not grateful to him. I am cringing under a load of obligation. And he is a tragic figure, and haunts me. Now to Mrs Merry I am just healthily grateful. And to Miss Basden my gratitude is quite of a brisk, employing kind. I almost feel more kindly to Mr Burgess, who has to have the opposite of gratitude, though I never quite know why. Now I must go and ask Mrs Merry if we may ask you to stay to dinner. I always think Nicholas and I carry that off so well, having to ask permission to have guests.'

'How Emily runs on and on, doesn't she?' said Herrick. 'Day after day, year after year, the stream never runs dry.'

'It doesn't seem that it could,' said Masson, 'that Emily could ever be subject to age.'

'I always wonder if she had any youth,' said Bumpus, his eyes sweeping over Masson. 'She seems somehow ageless, to have nothing to do with age.'

'You knew her when she was young,' said Herrick. 'But you were young too, then. She was wonderfully like what she is now. No, I think in a sense she had no youth, just as in a way she will have no old age. She is of that type. A rare one.'

'I think the two omissions compensate for each other,' said Masson.

'I do not. I like the whole of experience,' said Bumpus.

'I always wonder,' went on Herrick, in the tone of a man who kept back nothing of his heart, 'if I should have been happier or unhappier without her. I am never bound by convention, and the question arises in the case of any intimate relationship, however good. We could all have moulded ourselves differently.'

'We can't change the stuff in the mould,' said Masson.

'And Emily is a woman with a good deal of the man in hers.' said Bumpus.

'Oh, I have had more to do with women than you two have,' said Herrick. 'I am not as much off the common line. But most of my life's relationships have been with men. But that is what I meant. I wonder what I should have been, if I had not had Emily. And, William, you are thinking, what would she have been. But I am never the slave of convention.'

'Don't stop,' said Emily, returning. 'I like talk that is unfit for me. It is having to get used to Nicholas, who is not the slave of convention, as he says. Fancy being able to say that truthfully!'

'I believe in the interest of oneself, you know,' said Herrick, going on as if he had not heard his sister. 'I take the deepest interest in myself, apart from egotism of personality, though I may have that. And I have no condemnation for egotists. I think they are often the higher type.'

'This is not the kind of unfitness I meant,' said Emily. 'It does sound wicked, but not with a wickedness that I like.'

'I think on the whole they are not,' said Masson.

'You could not be an egotist, William, whether or not you wanted it,' said Bumpus.

'Surely everybody would want it,' said Emily. 'I am sure it would be dreadful not to be one. Isn't it, William?'

'Egotism is a gift, like anything else,' said Herrick.

'Then I grow prouder and prouder of you, darling,' said Emily. 'An author and an egotist, and both of them such lovely things.'

'I suppose your book is a novel, Herrick? Mine is,' said Bumpus.

'Yes, yes. A short novel,' said Herrick. 'I hold no brief for long books, as I say.'

'Real books coming out of our own heads!' said Bumpus. 'And not just printed unkindness to other people's.'

'My first original piece of writing!' said Herrick. 'That I should have to say it at seventy! Not just what Richard has said. Ah, I have felt that. Not that I have not done good work in that way. And it all has to be done. But my first book. Probably my only book, though many would be surprised to hear me say so. I thrill like a youth at the thought of seeing it out.'

'Oh, so do I,' said Emily. 'But not like a youth. Though I should love to do that once again. And it is better and safer at seventy. It will have to have the respect due to age, anyhow. But I am afraid Mr Merry will think it is a story book. Perhaps we had better keep it from him.'

'He must know about it when it comes out,' said Masson.

'No, I don't think Mr Merry knows about books when they come out,' said Emily.

Masson and Bumpus returned to the college, entered Masson's rooms, and sat for a time in silence.

'Well, William,' said Bumpus, 'I have protested that I have written a book. You must know that it is your part to seem to want to talk about it.'

'If you would like to talk of it with me,' said Masson. 'I think that men who take only to science, cannot be on the point enough in these things to be bearable.'

'I suppose you will not read it,' said Bumpus. 'Or if you do, will not tell me what you think of it.'

'Am – am I of the sort to read it?' said Masson. 'I hesitate, as I say, to inflict the alien touch.'

'It is this that thirty years has brought us to,' said Bumpus.

'I – I think it is a good thing to come to, to keep to,' said Masson, his voice going high. 'I think it is the worst thing about intimacy, that it may blunt every edge.'

'Yes, yes. Edges are the only thing,' said Bumpus. 'It is odd about Herrick, isn't it? His writing a book.'

'Odd, is it?' said Masson. 'Oughtn't he to have written before?'

'That does seem to me the alien touch,' said Bumpus.

'Well, perhaps it will hardly be a good book,' said Masson.

Bumpus laughed.

'I should have said that Herrick knew too well for that. He has his hand on his name with great skill. "Oughtn't he to have written?" That is what he has done. I don't follow. It is certainly odd how both he and I seem to have come to it suddenly. It is dwelling on the time when I sacrificed my other book, that had brought me to it. My mind has been on it lately. I don't know why I should be sensitive about it. My feelings had nothing in them to be ashamed of. This book seems to start out of all that, somehow, to go on from it. Well, there is nothing between.'

'In that way,' said Masson. 'You – you feel deeply about the book, Richard?'

'Yes,' said Bumpus, leaning forward, looking small and tense and alive. 'I have wanted to write all my life, felt it was this, it was mine to want. And it seemed not to come to me, after the early time when things happened as we know. There seems to be one book in a good many of us. And of course, that one book of mine was mine no longer.'

'No, no,' said Masson, not raising his eyes.

'So this means much to me,' said Bumpus, looking at Masson.

'It – it means then much to me,' said Masson. 'Perhaps Herrick's book is the one book in him that is in many of us.'

'No,' said Bumpus, laughing. 'I have more than one in me, and Herrick has not one at all.'

'Then the book must explain itself,' said Masson.

'I believe I am capable of any meanness,' said Bumpus suddenly, 'short of actually cheating people of their own.'

'Is there much meanness short of some form of that?' said Masson.

'No, no, none that matters,' said Bumpus.

3

The Reverend Peter Fletcher was a frail little elderly man, with a long, black beard, and a colourless face that carried a humorous kindliness. His wife, Theresa, was a large old woman, with fierce eyes looking out between a massive brow and chin. His sister, Miss Lydia Fletcher, was a clumsy-looking woman of sixty, with a broad, fat, benevolent face, and the Reverend Francis Fletcher, a nephew, was an oversized, youngish man, with solemn eyes.

'Say grace, Peter,' said Theresa, looking up from carving.

'I have just done so, my dear,' said Mr Fletcher.

'Peter, you see the result of thirty years of your example,' said Bumpus, who was a cousin of Mr Fletcher's, and gave an impression of a faint Fletcher likeness embodied in a great difference.

'I think it is a beautiful result,' said Emily, who was a friend of Theresa's. 'Fancy just not noticing grace after thirty years!'

'Being so free from nervous hurry at the least,' said Bumpus.

'Oh, one does not offer oneself as an example to one's elders and betters,' said Mr Fletcher, giving his peculiar smile, in which he stretched his lips without parting them, so that his teeth were not displayed.

He was nine months younger than his wife.

'Ah, it is so difficult to have the control of oneself,' said Miss Lydia, in a mysterious undertone, with her hand over her mouth. 'It seems that nothing is so small that we can do it without asking help.'

'Theresa does everything without help, doesn't she?' said Bumpus.

'Of course nobody who does that, could do quite actually everything,' said Emily.

'No. Not without help, no. Without always asking help, perhaps,' murmured Miss Lydia. 'For we can't do things without help. No.'

'Is the farewell sermon ready, Peter?' said Theresa.

'A farewell sermon! I do hope you had help,' said Bumpus.

'A life of work, and extra work to round it off!' said Theresa.

'Lyddie, is it ready?' said Mr Fletcher.

'The sermon is not my province,' said Miss Lydia, firmly on the truth.

'But couldn't it be with help?' said Emily. 'Oughtn't you to get particular help, being inside things as you are? Or is everything just coldly fair?'

Miss Lydia looked at the table.

'Aunt Lyddie is to do the work to the end, isn't she, Uncle Peter?' said Francis.

'Yes, yes, surely,' said Mr Fletcher.

'It is not a woman's business to preach,' said Miss Lydia.

'Of course not,' said Emily. 'I did not think of that. I didn't mean I thought it was.'

'Is it done, dear?' said Theresa.

'I have mapped it out in outline,' said Mr Fletcher, leaning back with his fingertips together. 'I have still two or three matters to look up.'

'You are self-important, Peter,' said Bumpus.

'Well, with a farewell sermon, that is just being open and above deceit,' said Emily.

'I shouldn't trouble about it,' said Theresa. 'The people who will hear it have never troubled about you.'

'I should denounce them at the last,' said Bumpus. 'No, I should not. I should be very subtle and aloof.'

'I do envy you for retiring,' said Emily. 'Fancy, if Nicholas could give up the school!'

'Ah, he is needed,' said Mr Fletcher.

'Oh, he is not, Peter,' said Emily. 'You should not have little ways of making yourself popular.'

'There is a great deal of ritualism in the town,' said Miss Lydia, rolling the 'r'. 'A great deal. It is so much we have to fight against. But we must be so thankful that we are allowed to do something.'

'The other side seems to be allowed to do more,' said Theresa. 'I hope they are more thankful.'

'Lyddie,' said Bumpus, 'have you been told about Theresa's being made on purpose without charity, because of the double share of Peter, with whom she was to become one?'

'Ah, but these ritualists do harm. They do harm. They are not right. It is idolatrous,' said Miss Lydia, looking in front of her.

'The true reasons for the simpler service have possibly never reached them,' said Mr Fletcher.

'No, no, Peter, keep a hand on yourself,' said Bumpus. 'That does not extend to us. We are more of a credit to you than that.'

'It is certainly time that Peter retired,' said Theresa.

'Where do your boys attend church?' said Miss Lydia to Emily, in a mysterious, piercing whisper.

'My boys?' said Emily. 'How nice of you! Because that is the impression we wanted to make. At the chapel on the college where Nicholas used to be. Richard's college.'

'Merry arranged it as a reminder to people that Herrick was a fellow there,' said Bumpus.

'You are very nice people to be employed by,' said Miss Lydia, her voice suggesting unworthiness in Mr Merry.

'Yes, we try to be grateful,' said Emily. 'It is so generous to be employed. Nicholas and I really have to shirk our part of it.'

'Mrs Merry is a good religious woman?' said Miss Lydia, raising her eyes but not her head.

'Yes. That is what she is. You are wonderful at descriptions.'

'I am sure, Aunt Lyddie, that Miss Herrick's and Mr Herrick's influence is everywhere in the school,' said Francis. 'I have so often heard about it in the town.'

'I wonder if that is all right,' said Bumpus. 'Are we quite sure what Merry wants about that?'

'Mr Merry is very happy in having no place in his life for criticism at all,' said Miss Lydia.

'Very happy?' said Emily. 'I think it would be unhappy and difficult. And we can't take everything, and give what is less than nothing. And that is what criticism seems to be. Peter, you do make me so jealous, sitting there. I wish Nicholas had a beard, and a kinder expression.'

'Sixty-eight years behind him, and not a respectable grey hair to show for it!' said Miss Lydia.

Mr Fletcher passed his hand down his beard.

'Wouldn't vanity seem to you a feeling incongruous with your calling?' said Bumpus.

'It would lack, I fear, what may be regarded as its necessities of life,' said Mr Fletcher.

'I wish I had said that. I mean, I wish I had thought of it,' said Emily. 'I mean, I wish I had thought of it just as a cleverness.'

'You see why he will not button his coat,' said Bumpus. 'It would be taking thought for what he puts on, when he is provided as the lilies of the field.'

Francis looked grave.

Theresa rose and rang the bell.

'My dear,' said Mr Fletcher, half rising himself, 'why can you not say when you want a thing done?'

'I do it and get back before anyone else is out of his seat,' said Theresa.

'It is unworthy of you to expect people to be prompt,' said Bumpus. 'Such a cold, self-esteeming way to be.'

'I am cold and self-esteeming,' said Theresa.

'It occurs to me,' said Francis, sinking back into his chair, 'that it was just so with my mother. She used often to vex and grieve me, if it had been possible for me to be vexed or grieved by her, by doing for herself those little things that I should have liked to do for her. I used often to reason with her about it, but she always refused to hear reason.'

'I must just trot across to the post,' said Miss Lydia. 'I have had to write to all my men, and tell them that my men's class will not be held on Thursday. Dear souls, they will be so disappointed, but I could not help it, or I would indeed.'

'Let me go for you, Aunt Lyddie,' said Francis.

'No, I am a person who does my own business. And this business is mine. I am so sad to disappoint my dear men things, who understand me so. I don't often fail them. Not often. And I don't often fail with them. I know I am different with women. I admit it. But men don't often elude me. Not often.'

'I feel I do elude Lyddie,' said Emily. 'I am always having proof that I am the average woman. And Nicholas has taught me to despise it.'

'She seems very pleased with not failing with men, and failing with women,' said Theresa. 'It would be better not to fail with either.'

'No, if you think a minute, not so good,' said Emily. 'Not so nice, anyhow.'

'I don't think myself so good,' said Bumpus. 'Much less good, of course.'

'It is something not to fail with one, my dear,' said Mr Fletcher.

'I knew you would say that, Peter,' said Theresa. 'You self-righteous, obvious old man. I did not say it was not.'

'Be patient with me, my dear. I shall be older and wiser presently.'

'You will be older and not wiser. At our age people get less wise.'

'Yes, that is true, my dear. I shall do my best for you, when the time comes for you to consult me generally.'

Mr Fletcher's eyes took on a look of grateful content, as the door shut on the women. He welcomed a man's companionship, and his friendship with Bumpus gave to his days a hidden light.

'I have been longing to have a word with a woman,' said Emily, sitting down with Theresa. 'Nicholas is so terribly a man. You must find that with Peter, too.'

'Sometimes,' said Theresa.

'Only sometimes?' said Emily. 'Yes, that is true about Peter. Nicholas is always a man. Life is just labour and sorrow for us. Labour for Nicholas and sorrow for me. You wouldn't think that Nicholas would labour. But lately he has. His way of writing this book is so like what an ordinary writer's, a real writer's way would be. He says it is ready in his head. Nicholas can't be like that. He says it came suddenly to him, when he was sitting up with Mr Crabbe. But he must have had it in his mind, and he has given no sign at all. And Nicholas ought to have given so many signs. It can't mean anything. Do you think him aged lately?'

'No, no, darling,' said Theresa. 'Particularly well and cheerful.'

'That is being so pleased that he is going to be conspicuous and highly thought of,' said Emily. 'He likes that much more even than the average man. In some ways Nicholas is built on a very large scale. I do hope it is all going to come off. I can hardly tell you how I hope it. He will be terribly shaken if it does not.'

'Well, why shouldn't it?' said Theresa. 'I wonder he hasn't done it before.'

'So do I,' said Emily. 'So does he. That is just it. At least, I don't think I do, really. I shouldn't have thought that Nicholas could write a book. Not a good book, not even just good enough.'

'Does your brother know what a good sister he has in you?' said Theresa.

'No,' said Emily. 'He knows what a good brother I have in him. How I should have had to go on the streets, or even be a governess, without him.'

'You had your own income, dear,' said Theresa.

'A hundred a year,' said Emily. 'Nicholas is kind, and without true dignity. He gives all his attention to one side.'

'You are very devoted to him?' said Theresa.

'You know how I feel to him as well as I do myself. How utterly I see through him, and yet know how necessary he is to me. And how pathetic. It will break my heart if this wretched book goes wrong.'

'Does he feel the same to you? As strongly, I mean?'

'No,' said Emily. 'You know he does not feel strongly like that about anyone. He is rather glad he has me. But he has a feeling that without me he would not have kept a school, and would have been a real writer. I think it might break him up if anything were to happen to me. You know that means if I were to die.'

'He only gives about ten minutes a day to the school,' said Theresa.

'Well, he couldn't give any more,' said Emily. 'I did not know you were one of those people who talk about Nicholas' ten minutes. And he doesn't see the other side. I told you.'

'Have you pointed it out to him, dear?'

'You know that would not make him see it. Apart from the way he already sees it. And I believe it is good for him to feel himself a kind of hero. It holds him up from going down into old age.'

'What would he do if you got married?'

'Live with me, I suppose. As a sort of upper husband. And look down on the other one.'

'My dear, if you are going to do it, it should be soon, shouldn't it? And, as you say, your brother could live with you.'

'You know I did not say it,' said Emily. 'And as if taking some of my attention! You can't be as unobservant as that. And if I can marry now, I can marry at any time. There is not much dependent on youth left at fifty. And William gets older at the same time. I don't pretend I don't understand you. I am not at all commonplace.'

'There is no one else, is there?' said Theresa.

'You should not actually talk to me as the average married woman thinks of a spinster.'

'Do you ever give him a chance?'

'Give William a chance? I see him every day.'

'But alone, dear? So that he is a free man?'

'In the room that Nicholas and I share, with Dickie looking on. Where else could I see him? The boys' basement dining room wouldn't make any difference. He couldn't propose to me.'

'Why not?'

'Why, I should think he couldn't. I haven't thought about it. I should think it is one of the things he doesn't do. We all have them.'

'But you could manage yourself, dear. People can,' said Theresa.

'Yes, of course they can. I've noticed that. And he would accept me, I am sure. I know he would spare me embarrassment. Dear William!'

'But he wants to marry you, doesn't he?'

'As much as he can want to marry anyone. Anyone who is a woman. And that is not very much.'

'Oh dear! These dons and people!' said Theresa.

'Yes, it is something of that way. I knew you knew all the time. I might tell you it is that way with me too. But I shall not tell you any more. Especially as you are ordinary and know it all. I understand now why people sometimes murder people they are known to be fond of. They ought to murder them.'

'Suppose you outlive your brother, dear?'

'Suppose I outlive him! Why of course I shall outlive him. I am twenty years younger than he is, so I mean to live twenty years after him. Don't you think a woman ought to live, if there isn't a man making use of her?'

'I thought you might not find things worth while without him. You said he would break up without you. I shouldn't like to live for ever, myself.'

'Yes, so I expect he would,' said Emily. 'But then I join him in living for himself. He doesn't join me in anything like that. I should love to live for ever. I don't wonder that religious people, who can plan things, arrange it like that.'

'No, but you might not miss him the less for that,' said Theresa. 'We miss what we give most too, the most.'

'I do not,' said Emily. 'I should miss him the less for that. But I should miss him. That is why I want this book to come off, so as to give him a new start of life. And I should live in a nice little house, if he died. Mr Merry would have the school, and make me an allowance. I might have two sitting rooms, and I should get so muddled between them. Where could William propose to me then? Though of course the school might not pay without Nicholas. People do admire him so for giving no time to it. It was so clever of him to think of it. Anyone else might have thought it would pay better to give all his time to it.'

'Darby and Joan gossiping together in the dark!' said Miss Lydia. 'Gossiping and gossiping away in the dark.'

'Well, the dark can soon be remedied,' said Theresa.

'Yes, yes, it is not incurable,' said Miss Lydia, feeling for matches as one wont and willing to do all to be done. 'It is not incurable, that is one thing. Not like the dark in the room I have just been in, a room under some stairs, with no light, and no fire, and some little children. Oh, dear! Something must be done. It must be done. How thankful we ought to be!'

'With a little less, we should be in the dark and cold too,' said Theresa. 'You could find people better for preaching thankfulness too.'

'Oh, no. For some people never know how nice it is to help,' said Miss Lydia. 'We ought to be so sorry for them. Because it is so nice. It is so nice.'

'Perhaps the people are pretending distress out of kindness to you,' said Theresa.

'No. People are not so difficult in their kindness,' said Emily. 'And they wouldn't guess it was nice.'

'Out of kindness to themselves then,' said Theresa.

'No, no. Not in this case. No,' said Miss Lydia. 'The man has struggled to get work until he is hopeless, just to get work, just that, poor soul! Hopeless and distrustful of everything. He hardly trusted me at first. But he does now, dear fellow. Dear fellow, how he does!'

Miss Lydia went to her desk, and stood with her knuckles on it, her eyes looking into space. The matter seemed not long without light for her, for she hastened towards the door.

'What a good soul she is!' said Mr Fletcher, smiling, as he came in from seeing Bumpus off in the hall.

'A soul who ought to be good,' said Theresa. 'No family, and an income of her own! She could not spend every penny she has on herself.'

'She could not, but there are people who could, my dear.'

'I could,' said Emily. 'I do.'

'Well, it is not for us to admire this dropping of driblets,' said

Theresa. 'We had half we had swallowed at one draught. That was a thing, if you want one.'

'I wish I had the use of vigorous metaphor,' said Emily.

'My dear, we did not intend to give it,' said Mr Fletcher, who had lent his inheritance, and failed to recover it.

'No. And so we had all the giving and no gratitude. That would not suit Lydia.'

'You know,' said Emily, 'I hate to say it, but I believe it would not suit her as badly as most of us. But very badly, I hope, of course.'

'It did not suit us, did it, Theresa?' said Mr Fletcher. 'I fear we murmured. I fear we did.'

'How conceited you are! Of course you did,' said Emily. 'I wonder if Lydia would not have spoken about it. If so, what a good thing she did not lose it! We should have had to admire her.'

'It is a good idea to leave debts unpaid when you die,' said Theresa.

'Very good. I will tell Nicholas about it,' said Emily. 'He very likely has not thought of it. He is really much more honest than people think. And he does not think he is going to die. And of course he is not.'

'My dear, he felt it more than we did,' said Mr Fletcher to his wife. 'And we have been a happy old pair without it. Though I don't know why I should call myself old, except that I like to be coupled with you, my dear.'

'I do wish I were not a spinster,' said Emily. 'I retract all that I have said.'

'Of course, Lydia flirts with her men,' said Theresa. 'She may not know it, but she does.'

'I wish I could do difficult things without knowing it,' said Emily. 'I always know, when I do them, so clearly and conceitedly.'

'Well, that kind of thing must be at the bottom of most things,' said Mr Fletcher. 'It may as well be put to a good purpose, whether or not people know it.'

'Peter, you really are rather like other people sometimes,' said Emily, 'though I don't like to belittle you before Theresa.'

'Emily, you are sometimes severe,' said Mr Fletcher.

'And that is like other people, isn't it?' said Emily. 'But why should you want not to be like other people, when you are a good man?'

'I do not want it,' said Mr Fletcher.

'Then why am I severe?' said Emily. 'But you are right not to let us speak wickedly about Lydia. It must be terrible to do good.'

4

'Now, I don't know how it is,' said Mr Merry, 'but you all look half-dressed, and in a state of slovenliness, somehow. I can't understand how it is that my boys cannot manage to look like gentlemen. Now, whatever is it so scrappy and untidy about you all?'

'We are to dress again, sir, presently,' said a boy, 'before the prize-giving!'

'Dress again, presently, before the prize-giving! Dress again, presently, before the prize-giving! Dress again, presently! And so it is not worth while to come down looking like gentlemen, though there are five or six hours before the prize-giving begins! Have any of you washed this morning, pray? Have you washed, Johnson? Have any of you said your prayers? Or have you put them off, till you shall be in church in four days' time? I have never heard of such a thing.'

'Miss Basden told us to – to do those things, and then not very much. We are to change all our things again presently. Miss Basden said –'

'Miss Basden said! Miss Basden said! You are a lot of boys to require a lady to come and say that kind of thing to you! Have you no gentlemanly sense of decency? Have you no self-respect? Have you no…? Oh, I have no patience to talk to you. I cannot understand it. I cannot. When I was your age… But get to your books, and let me hear no more of this dressing again presently because of the prize-giving. I cannot put up with it.'

A maid appeared with a request from Mrs Merry, that the boys would go down to breakfast directly they heard the gong, as there was no time to spare that morning.

'Yes! Oh, what, Fanny? Directly they hear the gong? Thank you Fanny, very much. Boys, you go down to breakfast directly you hear the gong. So don't stay behind to finish what you are doing, and to let me go out first, as I am forty years older than you, and your schoolmaster. I suppose Mother thought you would miss out hearing the gong this morning, as you have missed out most other things. And there is the gong! So rush down, and go stampeding like a herd of tatterdemalions who have never been to school, instead of gentlemen spending their lives in one.'

Mrs Merry was sitting before an empty tray, looking as if she had given up hope, except in smoothing her hair and glancing at the clock.

'Now, Mother, now, it's all right, Mother,' said Mr Merry, in an almost imploring tone. 'You are managing it all as well as it can possibly be managed. You know you are, Mother.'

'But it is not all right, dear. The cups cannot be done without. The boys have to have their breakfast as usual,' said Mrs Merry, almost implying that it would be only reasonable to waive this material start to the day.

'Oh, yes, ring the bell, Johnson,' said Mr Merry, avoiding looking at his wife. 'Ring the bell, Johnson, will you, please? Thank you, Johnson, very much. Oh, Miss Basden, good morning, Miss Basden. We were getting to feel all of a muddle without you.'

'You will have to feel all of a muddle again, very soon, then, I am afraid, Mr Merry. I have come in only to rush away again. Oh, the cups! I could not be there for once. No, Mrs Merry, I insist upon your not getting up. Mr Merry, will you please forbid Mrs Merry to rise?'

'Boys, go out and get your own cups for your own breakfast! Get up, and wait upon yourselves. When I was a boy, there was none of this sitting about of boys to be waited on. Oh, Fanny! Here you are, Fanny. The cups, Fanny, please. They have been forgotten somehow, in the bustle about everything today, you know. It is all right, Fanny. Thank you, Fanny, very much. Boys, be still, and don't first sit about to have everything done for you, and then when it is being done, begin to make a fuss. Can't you see that Fanny is getting the cups out for you now? Oh, you are a set of boys! Now, Mother, have a cup of tea, and let your mind rest, while you have your breakfast. Miss Basden, you do the same.'

'It is more pouring out three or four dozen cups of tea for other people, than having one cup myself, that I have to think about.'

'Yes, Mother, yes,' said Mr Merry, looking guiltily at the array of cups. 'You are always looking after three or four dozen people, it seems to me. But don't give up heart, Mother, you know. All days are not like today, you know. Why, Mr Burgess! How are you, Mr Burgess? Why, you look as fresh as if you were to have a prize. Ah! Anything out of the common is a great thing for you, isn't it, Mr Burgess?'

'Well, it depends upon how much it has to do with me, Mr Merry,' said Mr Burgess, who had come in brighter for the break in routine, but was already at his level. 'It sounds rather a confession, but I am afraid I had not thought of the boys' prize-giving. It was very self-centred of me.'

'It has brought you down in time, Mr Burgess, at any rate,' said Miss Basden, draining her cup on her feet.

'I had not thought of it, Miss Basden. But I am glad, if I have even unconsciously honoured the day.'

'Ah, Mr Burgess, it would not bring you down earlier, would it?'

'It appears that it has, Mr Merry. But it was an office performed for me quite without my own participation, as I say, though it seems these things are to be settled for me.'

'Boys, now, will you all be in your rooms by half-past eleven?' said Miss Basden, in a sudden, aloof tone, from the door. 'By half-past eleven, so that you can have done all you have to do, by twelve, when I shall come round and see that you are properly ready. Do you understand?'

'Can't any of you speak?' said Mr Merry. 'Can't you do something else than sit, when a lady makes kind proposals of this sort to you? What do any of you ever do for Miss Basden, that she should go round, when she has so much to do, and see that you are all ready? Now, thank Miss Basden, and say that, of course, you will be ready to the moment.'

'Fanny,' said Mrs Merry, 'will you remember that I shall want you all down in the basement this morning? So none of you are to be upstairs at all, after the rooms are done. Miss Herrick is answering the front doorbell.'

'What, Mother?' said Mr Merry, leaning to his wife. 'Miss Herrick, Mother? Miss Herrick answering the front doorbell! Why, is that necessary, Mother? Does Mr Herrick know about that?'

'Quite necessary, dear, or I should not have arranged it.'

'Yes, but Mother, Miss Herrick! Miss Herrick, you know! Why, I should not have thought that… I mean, is that all right, Mother?'

'Quite, dear. It is just a little arrangement between Miss Herrick and me.'

'Yes, mother,' said Mr Merry, with compliment in his tone towards his wife's relation with the sister of the head. 'But you know, Mother! Well, wasn't there any way out of it but that?'

'None at all, dear. Unless you can spare me one of the boys, to sit in the hall all the morning and answer the bell?'

'Oh, well, Mother! I don't mean that they wouldn't be a great deal more useful, sitting in the hall, and answering the bell, than doing anything they will be doing. For what will be the good of teaching them this morning, sitting patiently and trying to teach them, half dressed as they are, and their heads full of every kind of thing but what they ought to be full of? But you know,

Mother,' – Mr Merry spoke low – 'the parents, you know! If it got to them, all about being used, and missing a morning's work, you know! So I don't think, Mother…'

'Oh, of course I didn't really mean it, dear!' said Mrs Merry, half-laughing. 'And a boy would not be any good to me, really.'

'No. A boy would not be any good to you, really! A boy would not be of any good to you! Oh, wouldn't he? I am sure he would not. Now there is a thing to get about, about you all! Here is Mother, kind as she is, having to say that!'

'You might stay with the boys until they have finished their breakfast, dear,' said Mrs Merry, speaking with her hand on the edge of the table, 'and then get them out as soon as possible. We are not going to have prayers this morning so that the maids can get in to clear the room.'

Mr Merry waited with his eyes on the door, until it closed behind his wife.

'Not going to have prayers this morning! Oh! So you are to miss that out, are you, besides all the other things you have missed out today? It seems that the only things you are to have today are meals and prizes. I don't wonder that the custom of giving prizes is getting to be talked against. I don't wonder. And I tell you, there is one thing you will have this morning, and that is your work. So get up, and get out, whether you have finished your breakfast or not. "Stay with the boys until they have finished their breakfast!" Am I a nursemaid, or what? Why, Mother is all put about this morning. So get out, and get your walk and come back prepared to give your mind to your books. Do you hear me?'

'The end of breakfast is another thing that we can miss out today,' said Mr Burgess, implying personal indifference.

'Oh, well, Mr Burgess,' said Mr Merry, his eyes on the departing flock of boys, 'oh well, the boys needn't hurry you. But "stay with the boys until they have finished their breakfast!" Why, I shouldn't have dreamt of asking you to do it, Mr Burgess.'

Mr Burgess followed his pupils.

'Fanny,' said Mr Merry, 'this about Miss Herrick's answering the bell? Why, that is all right, of course? There isn't any way out of it? There isn't any one of you who could just run upstairs, you know, if you should hear the bell?'

'Well, no, I am afraid not, sir. Mr Merry's orders are that we are to keep downstairs this morning. There is a lot to be done down there.'

'Yes, Fanny, of course. Yes, Fanny. Thank you, Fanny, very much.'

Mr Merry went up to the hall, and catching sight of Emily, quickened his steps to overtake her.

'Why, Miss Herrick, here is our great day. Our great day for the lads, when we all work together, as you and Mr Herrick are so kind to us. And, Miss Herrick, you are so very kind to us. I hope there isn't any little thing you are doing for us today that will be a nuisance to you, you know?'

'Oh, no. Nicholas and I are just coming in, in our most beautiful clothes, when the people come. What could be nicer for us? And I am opening the front door, as we can hear the bell. But as the tradesmen go to the back and no visitors come in the morning, I don't know whom I am to open it to. Unless to Mr Burgess and the boys. That would sound good work, if I just said the number of people.'

'Yes, Miss Herrick,' said Mr Merry, making way rather hurriedly for Emily. 'Yes, Miss Herrick, very good and kind to us all. Oh, Mr Burgess! So you are not gone, Mr Burgess. Then make sure that you have your latch key, Mr Burgess, will you? Because there is a good deal of running about on people today, you know.'

'Yes, Mr Merry, I believe I have it. I always make a point of carrying it. A latch key is a useful thing to have on one, in case of wanting to run in and out.'

'Oh, well, Mr Burgess. Wanting to run in and out! Oh, well, just today I meant, you know.'

A few hours later Emily opened the door to Bumpus and Masson.

'So you are not ashamed of coming to see us when we are really helping to earn the living. I mean of being seen with us. Did you see Mr Burgess passing the college this morning, with his paper, and all the boys? How young did you think he looked?'

'About twenty,' said Bumpus. 'A nice boy.'

'Oh, you don't think he looks as young as that? Nicholas, here is Dickie saying that Mr Burgess looks about twenty, and a nice boy! And he is here to look quite apart from the boys. It is so worrying about the parents noticing how young he is. With Nicholas doing nothing, and Mr Merry's having no education, there is only Mr Burgess to be looked to for all the boys' advantages. Of course Miss Basden is better than all three of them. But parents don't count a woman.'

'That is unreasonable of them,' said Bumpus, 'as one out of every pair of them is a woman.'

'Perhaps that is how they know,' said Emily. 'But Mr Burgess only missed a year of college because he couldn't afford to be kept there, and he has been here eighteen months, so he really might be doing something now.'

'Has he no degree, then?' said Bumpus.

'Yes, he worked for it during the first year he was here.'

'I did not know you could do that for Oxford or Cambridge,' said Masson.

'I don't think it was Oxford or Cambridge,' said Emily. 'Don't be searching and snobbish, William.'

'Well, missing the culminating part of advantages does not show,' said Bumpus.

'Not very much to parents, I hope. It is only Mr Merry who really shows how much he has missed, and Mr Merry can do anything. Isn't it generous of him to spend his life giving to others what he has not had himself?'

'Why not hand over prayers to him, and retire, Herrick?' said Bumpus. 'If he can read.'

'It might be bold to make any change,' said Masson.

'And boldness in religion is out of place,' said Emily, 'when we have to be humiliated and lowly. Mr Merry can read. I saw him once, reading. But of course Nicholas has to read prayers. You must see that, Dickie.'

'Yes, yes. I see that, really,' said Bumpus.

'You were obvious, Richard,' said Masson.

'Dear Mr Merry!' said Emily. 'He is not obvious, is he? To support us all, so that people think it is Nicholas! I really don't think it is obvious.'

'It is in good taste,' said Herrick.

'You do your half, darling,' said Emily. 'It is all a matter of the time people take. There are those hundreds of helpless children, coming up from that cellar that we have never seen. I wish Dickens was alive, to expose schools. Mr Merry has stopped to look back at Mrs Merry, as if she were a dumb pet that understood.'

'I can understand Merry, too,' said Bumpus.

'I believe you can,' said Emily. 'That is a side I do so admire in you. We must go after them, Nicholas, and walk about, with you in your gown. It makes me feel homesick that Mr Merry shouldn't work any harder than the rest of us. And it is so humiliating that he hasn't a gown. I wish I could mend your coat, darling. It is really undignified for you to have your clothes mended by Mrs Merry, as if you were one of the boys.'

'They know we can't help him,' said Herrick. 'But Burgess can be helped, and he looks himself as if he wished he looked older.'

'Well, his heart is in the right place,' said Bumpus.

'And after all, they would know that we shouldn't have any-one really mature for him,' said Emily. 'But he copies Nicholas, so that they know that Nicholas' influence permeates the school, and that is bad. And then they ask, and find it doesn't, and that again is bad.'

'Fletcher is to give the prizes,' said Herrick. 'It has to be a parson. I don't know why.'

'Well, God does like reward,' said Bumpus.

'It is a great thing that Burgess at his age isn't a parson,' said Masson.

'It is a great success for him. I wonder if he thought of it, himself,' said Bumpus. 'Of course he did not have to think of it.'

'I wish Mr Merry did not look so affectionately at the boys,' said Emily. 'It makes Nicholas look so dreadful by comparison. And we don't realise how bad I look by Mrs Merry, so unmoth-erly. And suppose anyone should take Mr Burgess for a boy, or forget Miss Basden!'

'Does Miss Basden not like being forgotten?' said Masson, as one not disliking this himself.

'She is morbid about it,' said Bumpus. 'I have not spoken to her, but I can see that.'

'Don't be superior to women, and more so to those who earn their living, Dickie,' said Emily. 'It is so revealing of you. And not spoken to Miss Basden, when but for her you would have to support most of your nearest friends! You would find it so difficult to do it too. I believe Miss Basden does it.'

'Will there be a great crowd?' said Herrick.

'Well, we ought to want that,' said Masson.

'How generously you both identify yourself with us!' said Emily. 'Most of the parents are coming. I hope it doesn't mean that they want to look into things, or reassure themselves, or anything like that.'

'Will you make the speech on the spur of the moment, Herrick?' said Masson.

'Nicholas can't spend his genius on speeches for boys,' said Emily. 'He has his book to give it to.'

'People don't really make speeches on the spur of the moment,' said Bumpus. 'Merry will make it.'

'I thought an outsider always made the speech,' said Masson, 'that the schoolmaster's business was not to praise his own school, and all that.'

'You thought Merry's business was not that?' said Bumpus. 'Then what did you think his business was?'

'You know an outsider is not called in here to do anything,' said Emily. 'Mr Merry does it. And you should not call Nicholas an outsider, when our business today is to prove that he is not one. Now, we must go and serve under Mr Merry.'

'They also serve who only stand and wait,' said Bumpus.

'Don't notice it when you see Nicholas not being himself,' said Emily. 'His real self really doesn't do. And go up and shake hands with Miss Basden. And don't be arch and joking with Mr Burgess, as if he were young.'

Mrs Merry and Miss Basden were talking in easy tones, with a nervous unconsciousness of what they said.

'How do you do, Miss Herrick?' said Mrs Merry.

'Oh, Mrs Merry, what are you doing?' said Miss Basden.

'Poor Miss Herrick, to be forgotten!' said Mr Burgess, advancing to Emily with his hands under his gown, and drawing Mr Merry's glance.

'Oh really, Miss Herrick! Well! What am I doing? It is the idea of shaking hands with so many people.'

'Yes, Mother,' said Mr Merry, uneasily.

Herrick stepped on to the platform in gown and hood, his expression inviting attention to himself. Mr Burgess, conscious of his similar garb, took his place near him, and exchanged an easy word. Mr Merry, who had no right to a gown and hood, stepped up after them, and stood surveying his pupils with an air of fond understanding of boys.

'Now I am not much of a hand at speech-making. What I do is teach my boys, and be with my boys, and give all my time to my boys. But what I want to say to you all is, that I am glad to see you all amongst us today, that my wife is glad, and my kind helpers are glad, and Mr Herrick and Miss Herrick, whom you have really come to see, of course, are glad. In fact we are all glad to be together, to celebrate the good work done by our boys, by your boys, and by my boys, for I have boys, you know, though I have only girls, really, if I may be very Irish for a schoolmaster. And the prizes are not won only by those who have won them, you know, though that sounds Irish again, for we don't overdo things in the old-fashioned way, you know. So we will see the prize-winners take their prizes and the other prize-earners,' – Mr Merry glanced with tender pride round at the boys – 'show how glad they are that they have won them, which seems to be more Irish than ever.'

Mr Merry stepped down amid clapping from the boys. Mr Fletcher did his part with covert reference to a sheet of paper. The youngest boy presented flowers to Mrs Merry.

Mrs Merry took her stand behind a table furnished by a consistence of fate with cups and an urn.

'Well, Mr Merry,' said a father, 'so you haven't put my boy among the prize-winners? Of course I don't mean that. But he doesn't go in for taking prizes, does he?'

'Ah, your boy,' said Mr Merry, who knew the ill policy of honesty with parents, 'and a nice boy, too! No, he doesn't go in for taking prizes. No, not yet. But I tell you what.' Mr Merry's voice became intimate. 'If I had a boy, I should like him to be your boy. I will tell you that.'

Mr Merry passed on, and paused at Mrs Merry's table.

'Now, Mother, now, don't get all into a fuss, the result of all this will be that you are knocked up. I can see that.'

Mr Merry had not meant his words for the general ear, but had been more occupied with the feelings which prompted them, than caution in their utterance.

'Now, Mother, it is all right, Mother. You are just a little over-done. That is what it is. We know what it is. We don't think anything of anything.' Mr Merry referred in this way to the fact that Mrs Merry was in tears. 'It is just because you look after us all too well. That is what it is.'

'Well, Mr Merry,' said another father. 'And what have you to say for those two boys of mine?'

'Ah, the little fellows! My wife, she has a soft spot in her heart for them.'

'And how do they do at their books? John is a scatterbrain, I am afraid. I suppose these long holidays nowadays are a good thing?'

'Ah, little John! Well, some boys haven't the brains to scatter. And all work and no play, you know!'

'He would not like to be called little John,' said a grown-up sister, who was with the father.

'Wouldn't he?' said Emily. 'Not when we only keep them until they are fourteen! But the young are cruel.'

'Ah, Miss Herrick, you will talk in your way to us,' said Mr Merry. 'You know Miss Basden, do you not, Mr Bentley?'

'No, I think not,' said Mr Bentley, simply.

'Why, she is always here, Father. Every year,' said the daughter. 'How are you, Miss Basden?'

'She is always here. Every year with us,' said Mr Merry, lifting his hands on and off Miss Basden's shoulders. 'Always here, so that people don't notice her any more than they do one of ourselves. Because she is one of ourselves, if she will be, aren't you, Miss Basden?'

'You see the difference between ordinary people and Mr Merry,' said Emily to Bumpus. 'And you said you did not know Miss Basden. You rank with the ordinary people.'

'I always suspected it,' said Bumpus.

'Mr Herrick is just bringing out another book, is he not?' said Mr Bentley. 'Is it on any subject that the boys could get any – be interested in now, I mean?'

'Oh well, well, you know, if Mr Herrick wrote on a subject, then the book would not be his own. And that would not do for Mr Herrick. And writing for boys! Well, we could not expect that from him. But there is our atmosphere, our thing that we have to give, that other schools don't give. And that only Mr Herrick can do for us. Ah, and he does it for us. I wish I had it in my young days. Then I might not have been the schoolmaster now. I might have been the other thing. And I hope you ladies will be it. I do hope it. And, bless them, I shouldn't be surprised.'

Mr Merry wrung Mr Bentley's hand.

'Well, Mr Burgess, so you are going about, are you, Mr Burgess? Now what about this theory that we don't want long holidays? That is not quite on your line, is it?'

'Well, I dare say there is something in it, Mr Merry. When I first became a schoolmaster, I thought I should never get used to the breaks from work. But I confess I am becoming reconciled. That is the way of schoolmasters, I fear.'

'Oh, well, that is one kind of talk, Mr Burgess. But what would you have done, now, if you had not become a school-master?'

'Oh, you are off the point, Mr Merry.'

'Not at all, not at all. What would you have done, now, if you had not taken up school-mastering?'

'No, no, off the point, Mr Merry.'

'Mr Burgess seems deeply attached to the point,' said Miss Basden.

'It should attract even the humblest educationist, Miss Basden,' said Mr Burgess, bowing.

'Well, Mr Merry is an educationist, I suppose you will admit?' said Miss Basden.

'Surely,' said Mr Burgess.

'Ah, we understand each other, don't we, Mr Burgess?' said Mr Merry. 'With your kind help, Miss Basden, and you do for all of us.'

'Well, it wasn't quite so degrading as usual, was it?' said Emily, as the four settled into Herrick's study. 'Nobody spoke to me like an employer. Did anybody to you, Nicholas?'

'It went off admirably,' said Herrick. 'Admirably. I quite enjoyed it. I should feel quite proud of the school, as I thought a school a thing to be proud of. And Merry surpassed himself.'

'I saw you enjoying it,' said Emily. 'I saw you being proud of the school, too. That was charming of you. But I followed the workings of Mr Merry's mind too sensitively for enjoyment. A great mind on the rack would be a dreadful thing to enjoy. And he did not always surpass himself. He was really indefinite with Mr Bentley about his boys.'

'Oh, only with that kind of fellow,' said Herrick.

'How can you be so reckless?' said Bumpus. 'Or is that the attitude that makes for success?'

'With Merry behind, it will do,' said Herrick.

'We shall have to propitiate Mr Bentley,' said Emily. 'I am afraid it will not do, darling. Mr Bentley isn't so fond of your having Mr Merry behind as you think.'

'How will you do that?' said Bumpus. 'By having Merry qualify?'

'By asking Mr Bentley to dinner,' said Emily. 'Being for an evening with Nicholas teaches people better than anything. And it is difficult for them to behave like employers when they have been our guests. We ought to have him while the house is disarranged, and we will ask the Fletchers too.'

'Is a disarranged house better for dinner?' said Masson.

'Yes,' said Emily. 'This room has to be regarded as the drawing room, and a classroom made into the dining room, and the boys' basement dining room suppressed, to have anything at all. And Mrs Merry can't be asked to do that often.'

'No, no,' said Herrick.

'You will have to ask her about the dinner, darling,' said Emily. 'She never can speak to you, so she won't be able to say words of refusal.'

'Why cannot you ask her as often as you want, if she can't say words of refusal?' said Bumpus.

'You are so unmanly about Mrs Merry, Dickie,' said Emily.

'I feel rather unmanly about her,' said Bumpus.

'I feel unmanly in asking her this,' said Herrick.

'You think it is unwomanly of me to ask you to,' said Emily. 'But I have not the true courage that is womanly. It is being so much with me. But how you do realise the domestic problem, Nicholas! You are better than either Dickie or William at that. I think it must mean that you have the mixture of the feminine and masculine, known to be in genius. I feel so hopeful about your book.'

'Ah, Herrick, the time for our exposure gets near, doesn't it?' said Bumpus.

'Yes, yes, it does,' said Herrick. 'It does get near, indeed. And it will be something of an exposure for me. Because my book brings out really a new self in me, a self that I was hardly conscious was there, myself.'

'Yes, books do come out queerly in that way,' said Bumpus. 'Now my book shows an old side of me, a young side, I might say, that I thought had been covered up for twenty years. I wonder if any of you will find my old self in it.'

'I suppose that is the difference between an author and an ordinary man,' said Emily. 'Because of course there must be some difference. An author does things from a new self or an old self, and an ordinary man just from his ordinary self, as if he were doing an ordinary thing, which of course he is. I am glad Nicholas' is the new self, because his early one might not make a book quite suitable for a schoolmaster, for a schoolmaster to write.'

'Do you remember, how Herrick once said he could live without Emily?' said Masson, as he and Bumpus left the house.

'William,' said Bumpus, 'you know there is a thing I will do for you, if you want it done? If you want to marry Emily, it could easily be managed about Herrick. You might have to live with him. That would be easy. Or he could live with you. That would be easy. You are a rich man. I mean, I would bring the thing to Emily, if you would find less surface trouble so. I could bring her mind in turn to you. I would do my best, I would do well, between you.'

'Richard, I will say it to you,' said Masson. 'I am grateful enough, to understand you. I know what you think it might mean of change for you. I would accept it, if I needed it. I would take anything from you. But if I had wished to marry Emily, if she had wished to marry me, I will say the first, it would have been enough, I should have asked her many years ago. I should not have thought of Herrick, to be plain. I should ask her now, if the desire came to me. I should ask her myself, like the ordinary man I am.'

'Of course you would,' said Bumpus. 'I see it now. I never saw before. But I meant well. Oh, but I believe you know how well I meant.'

'I would take anything from you,' said Masson. 'But I would have you understand my feeling for Emily. I have all you supposed I might have for her. And I hope she has something for

54

me. I hope and believe it. For it means a great thing in my life for me. But you are the more necessary to me, as her brother is to her. That is not to say that you and he are exactly first to either of us. Do you see?'

'Yes,' said Bumpus. 'I think I always have seen.'

5

'Are the boys coming?' said the Reverend Henry Bentley.

'They are out of their room, Father,' said his daughter.

'I asked you if they were coming.'

'They are out of their room, Father. We are all a little late this morning.'

'I know we are late. I asked you if they were coming.'

Mr Bentley rang the bell, and took his seat. He was an upright, white-haired man in his fifties. He had been a parson and a younger son, and had come later into the family estate.

Two boys of twelve and thirteen edged into the room, with the words, 'good morning, Father'.

Mr Bentley simply turned his eyes on them, and the younger showed the behaviour natural to continual gratitude, by vaguely capering.

The daughter was a tall young woman of thirty, with a pointed chin, and a small, compressed, peaceful mouth. She was the child of Mr Bentley by an earlier marriage. He was a widower for the second time.

'I am sorry we are late, Father.'

Mr Bentley did not look at her. He bowed his head over the breakfast with an air of not sharing the general thanklessness. Delia raised her head a little after the rest. There was a suggestion about her of remembering their being late.

'We shall have a windy walk to the college chapel,' said Mr Bentley.

'What did you say, Father?' said Delia.

Mr Bentley did not answer.

'We shall have a windy walk to the chapel,' he presently said, in a still lower voice.

'What did you say, Father?'

Mr Bentley did not answer.

'Would you like lunch at one or half-past, Father?'

Mr Bentley was silent.

'Would you like lunch at one or half-past, Father?'

Mr Bentley was silent.

'Father, I think you heard me.'

'Since it is the fashion this morning to be deaf, I may as well follow it. I might ask how many people had heard me.'

'How late you were home last night, Father! Was the train delayed?'

'I walked from the station. The train was not delayed. It is not a distance one can walk in a minute.'

'You are so good in those ways, Father. We all ought to copy you.'

'I might as well not go on trying to do my best in any way, for all the attention that is paid to me. I am getting tired of things. I cannot say that I am not. And as for copying me, other people in my house certainly should not do less than I. John, if you cannot control your fidgeting, you must go. I cannot bear it.'

There was a long silence.

'Have you not a word to say this morning, Harry? Nobody would think that I went to the expense of sending you to Mr Herrick's to see you sitting there like a stock, as if you could not open your mouth.'

'No, I have nothing to say, Father.'

Mr Bentley looked round.

'Do not think of letting me keep you, Father,' said Delia.

'I am not able to think of it. I am going to my writing. I have a good deal to do before chapel. That will give you time.'

Mr Bentley's writing was held to have bearing on his property, and it gave him the position of the breadwinner.

When they were returning from the chapel, Mr Bentley spoke.

'An intellectual fellow, the chaplain. He gives you a sermon to think over, a sermon with some stuff in it. I dare say it is natural that the boys should not care to listen to him.'

Delia was silent.

'Really, I shall be glad when their self-absorption gets to such a pitch, that I am justified in closing my doors to them. I am beginning to feel that they have spoilt my home long enough.'

Delia was silent, and Mr Bentley turned back to the boys.

'Come, come, walk a little more briskly, as if you were not so utterly given up to self-indulgence. Ah! Self-indulgence is a thing I am not enough down upon in my family.'

When the lunch was brought, the elder boy did not see. Mr Bentley came to the table slowly, his expression unsympathetic towards any promptness.

'Harry, pray stop swinging your foot in that worrying manner.'

'Oh, I did not notice,' said the boy. 'Did you speak to me?'

'I do not think I did. I believe we have not spoken since we came in. But I wonder what kind of an experience it is never to be awake, or alive to anything outside oneself. I wonder what the result would have been, if I had spent my life in a state of lethargy, with no thought for anything outside myself. It would have been a nice thing for other people. Really, sometimes I get tired of denying myself, and wishing for nothing with my own life, and meeting simply with the kind of thing that I meet with.'

'Is it I who have brought this on everyone, Father?'

'Is it you? Oh yes, you are sure to be the prominent figure in your own view of anything.'

'I cannot alter my nature,' muttered the boy.

'Your nature! Even when you open your mouth, it is the same. You can, of course, adapt yourself to other people, as we all do, as I have done through my life, more than you could ever realise. If I had had visions about my nature, I do not know what would have become of all of you.'

There was again silence.

'What was the text, Harry?' said Mr Bentley.

Harry answered rightly.

'John, what was the text?'

John gave a start, and lifted his eyes to the ceiling, and his father looked away from him.

The family settled to books.

'What are you reading, John?'

John made a reply.

'I hope you are really reading it?'

'Oh, yes.'

'And what is your book, Harry?'

Harry rose and offered the book to his father.

Mr Bentley glanced at it, and went to his desk. His pen caught the paper.

'Another pen,' he said, turning his eyes on his elder son, but somehow held himself from the use of his name.

'Harry, are you deaf, and too self-indulgent to stir?'

There was a silence.

'Boys,' said Mr Bentley, his eyes still on his pen, 'you seem to make it a custom now to be with us on Sunday afternoons. I have said nothing of it that I can remember. As you are not of much good to anyone, I think we have perhaps had enough of you.'

The boys disappeared.

'Father, need you write any more today?' said Delia later. 'You will be quite tired before the week begins. Is it necessary?'

'Urgent business letters about the property which we are living on, are necessary. I should not have done any work today, if I had felt I could leave it.'

'Are you going to do anything tonight, Father?'

'No, I think I have done enough for one day, especially as I shall have to be up and about by seven o'clock tomorrow.'

Mr Bentley had chosen the morrow for an inspection of his estate, that is, he would rise to his duty while his family lay at ease.

'It is eight o'clock, Delia,' he said, as if the evening meal's not being ready to the moment was not to be conceived.

Mr Bentley carved as one not shirking daily burdens, by reason of a particular one about to fall on him.

'What were you doing all the time you were upstairs, Harry?'

'Oh, different things, Father.'

'What things?'

'Oh, just little, ordinary things, Father.'

'What things? You must know what you have been doing?'

'I have not been doing anything in particular. We were only upstairs a few hours, Father.'

'I do not require you to tell me how long you were upstairs. And I should like to know when you will do something, Harry. Just suppose that I spent my life without ever doing anything. There would be a very different life for you, to going every day to Mr Herrick's, and having money spent on you without any trouble for yourself. You would soon get to know the difference, very soon.'

Next morning, Mr Bentley came slowly down his staircase. He was late for his train, his reason for further delay. He walked to his place with an air of uncertainty whether to remain.

'Ring the bell, Harry,' he said, replacing a cover on a dish, and leaning back to read a letter.

'Is it too cold for you, Father?' said Delia. 'We kept on and on expecting you, and wondering whether to send it down to be kept hot. But I was afraid it would get too dry.'

'Your wondering whether to send it down to be kept hot, was not of much good, if you had made up your mind it would get too dry,' said Mr Bentley. He paused once or twice in his speech, and did not lift his eyes.

'I did not think you would be so long, Father. You were so nearly ready when I passed your room.'

Mr Bentley gave a casual glance at his daughter. He had done what remained with the utmost slowness, and a bitter sense of lookers-on.

'Take this down, and do me some fresh,' he said to the maid.

'Delia, can we go?' said Harry.

'Ask Father if he will excuse you,' said Delia.

'Father, can we go? It is past school time.'

'If it is past school time, why did you not ask to go at the proper time? Why ask at all, if not at the right time? And using that ridiculous voice, as if there were some benefit to me in your sitting there! You are here to satisfy your own appetites. Go, of course. I do not want you.'

Mr Bentley observed his sons as they left the room.

'I have never met a man so unfortunate in his children. Self-conscious, conceited, with the manners of clowns! Sitting there, thinking their society such a benefit, and then the first words they utter to do with themselves! Neither of them taking the trouble to say good morning to me, but speaking fast enough as soon as they wanted to get off to their own pursuits! It is unbelievable.'

'I do not think Harry is well. I think he has one of his head-aches coming. I have thought so all breakfast time.'

'And why did you not speak of it, if you saw it? Why did you sit there and take no notice of a child you knew to be ill? Really, Delia, I should not have believed it. It is a hard thing, a hard thing, a hard thing. I may not have done much to lead my children as I would have them go, but my example should not have led them to this. It should not.'

Delia rose and left the room.

Mr Bentley was about to follow her, when she re-entered, forcing him to pause. He stood with his head and arms so rigid that they shook. Delia edged by him, and stood with her eyes on his face.

'Come, speak, Delia. Do not be mysterious. It is the worst breach of manners. What secret can there be?'

'Can I speak to you, Father?'

'Speak? Of course you can speak. Do get out of this way of making mysteries. Speak, and try to be natural and to the point.'

'John and Harry have come home, Father. They want to speak to you, I think.'

'Want to speak to me! Want to speak! Of all the habits my family has ever had! Call them in, and let them speak, make them speak. I will have no more of it. It makes me too ashamed.'

'Let me pass, will you please, Father.'

'Oh, it is nothing that requires anyone to be put about for it. They have come back because they "want to speak", I believe. My children are fond of that plea.'

'Father, we must see if anything is the matter with them.'

'Harry! John! Come in at once, and tell your sister what you want with her.'

'Well, what is it that you have to say, that you have come home from school when the morning has hardly begun? Let us hear it, so that you can get back again. I do not like this easy breaking off for any reason that comes to hand.'

'I have a headache,' said Harry. 'Mrs Merry sent us home to tell Delia.'

Delia went out of the room with the boy.

'John, go after your sister, and come back at once, and tell me all about your brother. I must know if I am needed. I will put off my journey today.'

'You will not be needed. Harry did not even want you to be told.'

'Oh, you idiotic, self-absorbed children! Have you not reason to grasp, that it is what is good for Harry that has to be thought of? Can you not bring yourselves to some real concern for your brother? Must you go on, thinking of nothing but how things can be settled for you to see the least trouble? Oh, that I could get you to see it! But I have given it up. As I say, I will give up my journey today. I will be ready to hear what is best to do, and ready to do it.'

John gave a caper.

'You see, John, it is not always an easy thing to bring people to see what is right, when one is at the head of a household where people are fond of going their own way, whether it is the right way or not. It cannot be done, my boy, without much of what must seem to people who do not understand – and my family are people who do not understand, I am sorry to say – to be needless, and even trying. But you will look back upon what your father did, when I am no longer with you, and see that it was not done easily.'

John looked at his father with rising tears.

Mr Bentley just laid a hand on his head, and went upstairs and stood by himself, repeating his speech with additions which had not occurred to him.

When he went down later, he saw that his daughter had dropped a spoon she had brought from the sick room. He watched her look with a resolve not to help the search and sat down and opened the paper.

'Well, I have to go on under this fresh burden of anxiety. It is not an easy thing to do, for anyone who cannot sink at once into his own affairs. Ah, it is a sad thing in many ways to be wrought upon by things outside oneself.'

'I am sure we all feel about Harry. But he is not really ill. And it is hardly right to make a great trouble out of a little one.'

'You are a self-satisfied young woman.'

'Self-satisfied? Oh, you do not know me, I think, Father. And

I am sure I have no right to be self-satisfied. I am many things I should not be. I am quite conscious of that.'

'You are a wonderful young woman, to be conscious that you are not perfect.'

'I think we are all rather out of sorts, and strung up, so to speak, about it.'

'It is a great thing if Harry gets over this,' said Mr Bentley. 'It is hardly to be expected, I suppose, in such a case of neglect, though of course it is right to do everything as if we did not expect it.'

There was silence.

'Well, upon my word, you all make life very hard for a man. I do not know what I have done, that I should be subjected to this. Here I have done my best for all these years, gone on doing all I could do, never lost patience, never dwelt upon what I might have had. And now, because I try to keep a wise and firm hand over people for their own good, and to prevent them from sinking down, down, down, for their own sakes – whose, if not for theirs, I should like to know? – to be given as much to bear as if I were a tyrant and a monument of selfishness, instead of…! Oh, it will not bear discussing. Why should I discuss it? Some people have much from others, and some have nothing and give all. It is just that, I suppose.'

'There is John come in again from school,' said Delia. 'I will go out and tell him not to come in.'

Delia was capable of revenge.

'Oh, what does it matter whether he comes in or not?' said Mr Bentley, his eyes dilating. 'That is not the sort of thing to give our thought to now. It is not a time for thinking about nothing.'

Delia turned to the door.

'John,' called Mr Bentley, 'come into the room, and hear what there is to be heard about Harry. It is not right that you should

65

not hear of your own brother. I will have no concealments and associations on false pretences in my family. Ah! That is what makes family breaches. That is what leads to them.'

'Did you call me, Father? I had gone upstairs. I was not quite sure.'

'You heard me call, I suppose?'

'Yes, Father. That is why I came down.'

'Then I imagine you were sure. Really, John, you talk as if you were not in your right mind. I suppose, after all, you are too stupid, and childish for your age to be told anything, even what it is not right that you should not know. Go away, then. Go away to your own concerns. I will not tell you, then.'

At this point the maid brought in a note of concern from Emily.

'Do you see much of Mr Herrick and Miss Herrick?' said Mr Bentley, when he had read it.

'No, Father.'

'How much do you see of them? You know what I mean.'

'Not – not much, not at all, Father.'

'Do you see anything of anyone, may I ask? Does anyone have anything to do with you? Teach you, for instance?'

'Mr Merry, and Mr Burgess, and Miss Basden, and Mrs Merry, sometimes.'

'I think Miss Herrick is very charming,' said Delia.

'Oh, don't be so obvious, Delia. Don't be too obvious. We all know that. That is what made me ask about it. That is what it is, of course. Well, I shall have a very fair idea of what to say when we go to that prize-giving.'

As he returned from the prize-giving, Mr Bentley spoke.

'This wind makes exceedingly trying walking. We never seem to be without it now.'

'We do have it very often. I hope the boys will think to put on their coats to come home.'

'Oh, from that school? I expect that Merry will wrap them up, and watch them out of sight, to see that they do not step in the puddles. That is the sort of thing they are accustomed to there, I think.'

Delia was silent.

'I wish I could find a school for them more like the one I was sent to as a boy.'

'I do not think Mr Merry is as easygoing with them as he seems. I think that is just his little way.'

'I was not speaking of his being easygoing, or about his little way. I was thinking of his being such an unmitigated nincompoop. Such talk as his no sane man would credit, if he did not hear it with his ears. It is enough to ruin a boy to listen to it.'

'Mrs Merry is a nice woman,' said Delia.

'What difference does it make, whether she is a nice woman or not? That does not teach the boys, or help them to earn their living. And I do not know if Miss Herrick is a nice woman. I should think not. But I do know that she does not do either.'

They entered the house in silence.

'Whatever on earth are those boys doing? Palavering about, handing cups to people they have never seen! They are fonder of waiting on strangers than on their father.'

'They have to do it, Father. They do not enjoy it.'

'Do not enjoy it! It is the only sort of thing that John does enjoy. I wish I had sons more like myself.'

The boys came in.

'Oh, we have had the prize-giving! Harry has got his prize. We had to hand round the tea.'

'You spent a very long time in handing round tea. I spoke to Mr Merry about you both. He had not much to say for you.

'And you seem to have a great many friends at that school, as far as I can judge. Giggling, and talking, even while the prizes were being given away! It does not look as if you had no friends to ask to your home, as always seems to be the case, when I ask you why you do not bring them here, and let us have an idea what kind of people you are with, when you are away from us all day at such expense. There are very few of them who have been brought up as you have, I am sure of that. Anyone would think you would be proud to let them see your father and your sister and your surroundings. I can't think what makes you so affected and self-conscious about it. Now, once and for all, what is it?

'Well, do not speak then, do not speak. Go off to your own employment, and settle down by yourselves, and do not say a word to your father, who makes sacrifices all day, so that you may have every advantage, and was trying to arrange something else, that you might have further pleasure. Go away then, and do not speak. Behave as my children always do. Go away, without a word, to your own concerns.'

6

'I hope, Uncle Peter,' said Francis, 'that Mr Herrick and Mr Bumpus will excuse me for not being present at their literary inauguration. I have very little time to myself, and I am obliged to deny myself all recreative reading, and being read to must be counted under that head, I think. So, if you will make my apologies to the authors, I will leave you before they come in. Though I admit it hardly seems fair to deny myself as audience, as I am safe in that way myself. We clergymen have an unfair advantage.'

'Yes, the poor laity!' said Miss Lydia.

'The arrangement was just for Peter and me to hear the books,' said Theresa.

'Yes, yes,' said Francis, in a kindly voice. 'Then I may betake myself with a clear conscience to the solid pursuits which must be my portion, I fear.'

'I too must go to my solid pursuits,' said Miss Lydia. 'But the dear men things! How interested they have been in it all!'

'Well, listeners never hear good of themselves,' said Bumpus, coming in.

'But they don't often hear anything as bad as that,' said Emily. 'What are we to say? People don't speak about their own kindness, and of course it is kindness in Dickie and Nicholas to be going to read their books to us.'

'Ah, yes, yes, it is all for us,' said Miss Lydia. 'And we must not underrate the pleasure things.'

'Well, we shall not overrate them,' said Herrick.

'Could we overrate things of that kind?' said Emily. 'Well, are you going boldly to begin, or am I to work at leading up to it? I couldn't expect anyone else to do that. Peter admires you too much, and Lydia not nearly enough, and William and Theresa are above leading up to things.'

'Well, well, we might begin,' said Herrick.

'Yes, yes, begin, Herrick,' said Bumpus.

'Yes, it is your business, dear,' said Emily. 'Dickie is a relative, and has to be put last in everything. It would be presuming upon your intimacy with the house to hold back.'

'It is so nice to help in any way,' said Miss Lydia.

'I said that Lydia did not admire you nearly enough,' said Emily.

'She really admires us terribly little,' said Bumpus.

'Well, she has killed any desire in me, but to do my simple best in anything I may undertake,' said Herrick, opening his papers.

'Yes, we must keep Lydia here. She will put the right spirit into it,' said Bumpus.

'Oh, no, no, I can't be here. But it is so nice to be wanted, thank you, thank you. So nice to go off to what calls me most, feeling that I should be welcome at what calls me less, calls me too, though it does not need me. For it does call me. It does call me. But I must go to the need.'

'I am so proud of you for writing the book, Nicholas,' said Emily, 'and especially for going to be known to have written it. And so remorseful for thinking you might not be great, when you always hinted. But the great always forgive.'

'Well, well,' said Herrick. 'It came to me, you know, that night when we sat up in turns with old Crabbe. The whole thing came upon me, just through that little service to somebody else.'

'It was really too much reward,' said Emily. 'But of course you deserved it.'

'Why, Bumpus,' said Herrick, looking at Bumpus' papers over his shoulder, 'your beginning sentence is the same as mine!'

'The same as yours?' said Bumpus. 'Why, it can't be. It can't be, surely. Why, there wouldn't be anything in common in our books.'

'Dickie, don't say out what is in your mind openly to Nicholas,' said Emily.

'Why, what is there in an opening sentence?' said Herrick. 'All opening sentences are much on a line, aren't they? All books have got to begin.'

'Nicholas, you have had faith in yourself,' said Emily. 'Do let us get it over. Anyhow, you have one sentence as good as Dickie. So let us have the beginning. That may be the only part we can bear.'

'Yes, get on, Herrick,' said Bumpus. 'Your book is ready to the word, and mine isn't. You are a greater than I. You have your own mind in hand.'

'I have sympathy with boasting,' said Emily. 'I hope Nicholas has.'

'Yes, it is ready, Bumpus, it is ready,' said Herrick. 'It may be the last and only thing, but something it is at last. You may all like to remember the day, when you heard it from my own lips.'

'But don't spoil it for me by reminding me that I may be without a breadwinner,' said Emily, 'especially as you don't win any bread. Dickie is not doing things like that. I think I have proposed to you, Dickie. But we haven't time to go on about it now.'

'Mine is not such a one as this one,' said Bumpus. 'I have had some delay with it. I left it in old Crabbe's room the night he died, and it was got rid of with the other things. Crabbe's illness brought on your novel, Herrick, but it held back mine. But it is the better for the rewriting of it.'

'Old Crabbe's room? That night he died?' said Herrick. 'Did you leave your book in the room, did you say, Bumpus? Ah, yes, it was a sad night, that, for us. Good old Crabbe! I always wondered that he never wrote. I have often said it. Did you leave your book in the room, did you say, Bumpus?'

'He never wrote. Not a line,' said Bumpus. 'He was of a different kind. Yes, I left my only copy of it in the room, the typed copy, I always tear up manuscript, and it was cleared away with the other things. And rewriting it has meant reworking at it. You must make the best of it. I find I don't take up writing again so easily. My best went into that early thing. Well, I have told my tale. That is the better thing, there where it is. Not that that matters now.'

'Couldn't you write the early one again?' said Emily, keeping her face turned from her brother. 'You could make it come back to you. A book when it is written could hardly go. William and I are the only people Nicholas has no influence over. It makes me admire Nicholas, but not you.'

'Well, does one do that thing?' said Bumpus. 'Having done the other. Besides, that sort of thing comes and goes, and then exists of itself, if has got on paper. But I confess I should like to be able to bring it out, and have the credit of it.'

'Exists of itself when it has got on paper!' said Emily. 'It was as good as that, was it? Then I wish you could have the credit of it.'

'Perhaps somebody could really begin to read it,' said Mr Fletcher.

'Perhaps it could read itself,' said Theresa.

'Emily, Emily!' said Herrick. 'Please forgive this sister of mine, Bumpus. She quite puts me off reading my own book today. She does indeed. We will just have yours. Anyhow, we will have yours first. Yours is not finished, so anything we don't like in it, we shall think is not going to be there. So it is easier for you.'

'Why should the first be last, and the last first?' said Bumpus. 'Mine will not bear hearing as yours will. My real book is where we know it is.'

'Why, yours will do as well, Dickie,' said Emily, 'much better, I am afraid. You can see that Nicholas is too frightened to read his, now that the moment comes. And perhaps it is a good sign. Good writers always feel a great wave of depression about their work, and Nicholas' symptoms were so bad. Yours are all right now.'

'Well, well, then, I will start,' said Bumpus. 'But I wish it were not this book that I was reading.'

'Richard,' said Masson, in a quick, expressionless voice, 'you know that copy of your other book, that you gave to me once, when you thought it was too illegible to be used? I think now is the time to tell you that I kept it. I put it by, before… when there was no question of the book's not coming out. And then I did not feel sure in taking on myself to destroy it. So I have it, if you can use it.'

'You have it? You kept the copy? That copy I gave you all those years ago, that I was going to burn? Oh, I remember now. You had not read it, had you? We were going to put it on the fire without your reading it?'

'I did not read it then,' said Masson. 'I seldom read any but scientific books, as you know, even my friends' books. I did not even in those days. But when it was to go, I read it, to have my own impression of something of yours. I knew I had been at liberty to read it. And then I could not feel sure in destroying it. I should not have spoken of it, had you not expressed a wish for it, and I had provided for it to be burned at my death. I may seem to have taken much on myself. But I was helpless. I felt I could do nothing else.'

There was a silence.

'Oh, well, I will look over it again,' said Bumpus. 'It may not be what I thought. But it is good news to me in a way. Thank you, William, thank you. I will try to use it, indeed. I will let this one go by for the time, and get the other out as soon as possible. After all, it is foolish not to change my mind when I really have changed it. And I have shown you all that I have done that.'

'Yes, even William,' said Emily. 'And it is such an opportunity for being above self-consciousness and convention and other things. It would be dreadful to waste it.'

'Well, I will not waste it,' said Bumpus. 'I would rather work on the other book. I couldn't deal with the two at once. I dare say it isn't as good as I thought. I was greatly younger then. But I don't feel I could go against you, William. Or myself, either. And I won't read this one today. This book will go to the wall for some time to come. Who ever had so good a friend?'

'And I won't read mine,' said Herrick. 'I too will wait for a future day. It wouldn't be a good thing now. I shouldn't take any interest in it, myself. My congratulations, my congratulations, Bumpus. I am glad, glad for you. I think you will always be the man of letters of us. I feel doubts about my own book after all. I feel a great wave of doubt about it. I believe I shall not have it finished for a spell of time. I believe I shall be like Crabbe, a man that all his friends think ought to write, and who never does. But I hope that like him, I shall encourage my friends.'

'No, no, no. What reason is there in this?' said Mr Fletcher. 'Why should we be baulked of the present books? You can read yours, surely, Richard, and then go on and finish it, before you get on to the other. And we must hear yours, Herrick, if not now, at some time very soon. Whatever has come to both of you?'

'I couldn't read this one today,' said Bumpus. 'William has put me off it, thrown me right back from it. I couldn't get the other out of my head. I must go straight on to it. I am on it at this moment, in my mind. I shan't be on this one again until the other is done. And it may have to be remodelled then, in the light of the old one. A man can't do his own books entirely apart. I may have got some of the one into the other. The old one was so much a part of myself. But I dare say it isn't so much good, really. I took things hard when I was young. Well, well, let us leave it all alone. How patient you all are! I must be getting away.'

'What insight we are getting into the minds of writers!' said Emily. 'No wonder they are not much good at things that can't so well be held up. Dickie and Nicholas have both proved that they are authors at heart. But what they are in any other way, we are not to know yet. Nicholas, you must work some more at your book, to make up for not having an extra one from your youth. It is such a pity you haven't one. It makes you so inferior to Dickie now, and it left you so much time then for other things.'

'Oh, I think I shall leave my books to chance, and interest myself in Richard's,' said Herrick.

'But are we not to have the books?' said Masson.

'You are not the one to complain,' said Emily. 'You have had one of Dickie's books to yourself, and no one else has had anything at all. And don't be out of sympathy with the erraticisms of genius, because no one should be too far removed from it.'

'We are carrying it off very shamelessly,' said Bumpus.

'Are you?' said Emily. 'That always seems to me the one thing authors are not, shameless. I think it would be better and safer for you to go, for fear we might bring it home to you. Peter and William were trying.'

'Two books in the hand, and now one in the bush,' said Theresa.

'Theresa, you are really the only genius here,' said Emily. 'Genius is spontaneous, and the genius of Dickie and Nicholas doesn't seem to be that. You had better go home, Nicholas dear, and leave Dickie and William on your way. You want a rest, and you can't get that with greatness about. Dickie is great intellectually, and William morally. Moral greatness is the best, though I have always wondered if that was true. And I am going to talk to Theresa. Peter will walk with all of you, won't you, Peter?'

'Isn't it your birthday today, dear?' said Theresa, as the two women were left alone.

'Yes, so it is,' said Emily. 'That is why I am out of spirits. I am fifty-one, and I don't much like getting to have so little life left. And yet I don't much like living, which is absurd, and makes it impossible for things to be planned for me, because what can be done?'

'You don't like living, dear?' said Theresa.

'No,' said Emily. 'Of course I don't like it. This has been the worst birthday of all the fifty.'

'What is it? What is it all?' said Theresa. 'I see something, and yet I don't know quite what to see.'

'Oh, Theresa,' said Emily. 'Did you see? Did you see? Nobody else saw? The men didn't see? I always thought I had a man's mind, but I must have a woman's instinct after all. At any other time, I should be ashamed of that.'

'You have nothing to be ashamed of, dear.'

'No, but Nicholas has not much,' said Emily. 'Why shouldn't he have a book, when Mr Crabbe was dead and didn't want it? Dickie found that a book wasn't any good to a dead friend. After thirty years of thinking about it, he found that. And what was Dickie doing, leaving a book about, when Nicholas wanted one so much, and couldn't make one for himself? And Dickie knew he couldn't. He always unkindly never deceived Nicholas about it.'

'Mr Crabbe?' said Theresa. 'Mr Crabbe? I only half understand yet. Was the book Mr Crabbe's? I thought it was Richard who left the book in the room? Oh, your brother thought the book was Mr Crabbe's? Oh, I see now. I thought he did not guess whose it was. I see now. I see.'

'Yes, that is it, I am sure,' said Emily. 'But do you see the other thing? Did you see about Dickie? That book that he left in the room, that he had to write again, was the same as his early book, that was buried with his friend! I believe it was. I am certain it was. Did you feel that, when William and he were talking? He couldn't begin his book, because William had read it. Of course I am not sure. But then I am. That is why Dickie is putting it away for the time. It is a good thing the book did not begin to read itself, as you said.'

'Oh!' said Theresa. 'There was only one book, then? All three were the same book? Your brother's and Richard's, and the other of Richard's that William kept? They were all just Richard's old book?'

'Yes,' said Emily. 'It sounds clever of Dickie, doesn't it? You wouldn't think that one book would have to go so far. Dickie and Nicholas were both wonderful about managing things. You wouldn't think they would find books so difficult. Poor Nicholas wanted a book so. And he knew Mr Crabbe was dying and friendless, so that no one could have read his book. And it was typed, so that he couldn't tell it by the handwriting. He thought it out so cleverly. Of course it makes it much worse of him. But perhaps he forgot all that. Criminals do forget something.'

'It was a shame!' said Theresa. 'So you think that Richard remembered his book, and wrote it again? And then again, after your brother had… had taken it?'

'Yes,' said Emily. 'He had a lot of trouble, hadn't he? But it was his own book. That seems quite good and strange of him. And worth the trouble, really. He was always saying how his book went back to his youth. He almost told us. He was really rather honest, considering everything. And William had read the book, which isn't like William. That must have been put into William's heart. Because of course Dickie wasn't doing quite rightly.'

'Suppose any one of them had begun to read it,' said Theresa.

'Oh, I was afraid you would begin to suppose that! To read it! How dreadfully you realise the thing! And your sinister notion that the book might begin to read itself! I believe in religion now, and about our never being given to bear what is beyond our strength. Anyhow, we shouldn't be on our birthday. If it had happened, Nicholas and Dickie and William and I, and Peter – but does Peter know? – could never have met again. And we none of us know anyone else.'

'Peter does not know,' said Theresa, firmly. 'What a thing for your brother that you have never married, dear! But I have often thought you would both be happier. Your brother married, as well.'

'Nicholas and I happier married! You don't think, Theresa. Wives can't think. Married people reveal all their past to each other, don't they? Peter must have had a lovely past. Nicholas couldn't do that. He hadn't ever a good past, not at marriage-able age. And he certainly couldn't now. And he is seventy. He would have to marry an old lady. And she would not like the noise of the school. And it would really be taking advantage of Mr Merry, because old ladies have so many little extra wants.'

'Does William suspect anything about the books?' said Theresa.

'No, they none of them saw anything. Even Dickie and Nicholas each thought he was the only bad one. But they had enough to think of. So I know for certain that I could never marry William. For I find that I only like wickedness and penetration.'

'Shall you tell your brother that you know? Does he know you know?' said Theresa.

'I shall tell him nothing. If he thinks I know, or may know, we just shall not speak of it. Then that will be the same to him as my not knowing. Nicholas is like that. And what is adorable to him, is that he would think no less of Dickie. He never despises baseness. That is why it is so right of him to be base. I should appreciate him better, and owe him more, if I were more base.'

'No, it isn't much good to you, dear.'

'No,' said Emily. 'That is what I am saying. It hasn't been quite fair to Nicholas.'

'Shall you tell him about Richard? Does he suspect?'

'I think he is not subtle enough, and was too absorbed in his own affairs. No wonder. Of course I shall not tell him. It is no business of mine. I am not even sure. I ought not to have said a word to you. I knew you couldn't really know. They are none of them as base as me. I am quite a chance for Nicholas, if only he knew. But you won't say a word, Theresa? Not a word.'

'Oh, no, dear,' said Theresa.

'I think I can trust you,' said Emily. 'I know you don't mind that kind of wickedness. So why should you reveal it?'

'What an extraordinary thing that they didn't give themselves away!' said Theresa. 'It all fell about in such a minute, too. It almost seems as if something must have been there to prevent it.'

'Hardly anything providential,' said Emily. 'They couldn't be thought to deserve that. But you and I certainly didn't deserve its being spun out. Nicholas was afraid to read a thing that he couldn't have written. Because of course he couldn't have written Dickie's book. He was always leading up to the shock of it. And it was natural for Dickie to tell us that he had had to rewrite his book. All that rewriting would have to make an impression. It was really unlucky that he hadn't told us before. Things always happen so hardly on Nicholas.'

'But Richard might have begun to read his book,' said Theresa. 'It was only William who by chance prevented him.'

'Yes,' said Emily. 'If we are to persist in thinking unproved evil of Dickie, and of course we are to do that. That must have been providential, and I told you I had got religion from it. So organic too, for William to prevent it, when it was only he, who had made the prevention necessary! William couldn't have been so egotistic by himself. This may have happened to convince you how far he and I are from each other. Providential things seem to be circuitous, like that.'

'I can't think why Richard couldn't have said that his book was the old one,' said Theresa.

'When one book was so much above the average, too,' said Emily. 'But he didn't know it was. He thought it was being just equal to Nicholas, and that has never done for Dickie. Did you see the shock he had in thinking one sentence was the same? I wish my shock had only been that. And then there was going back on what he had done. That was the trouble. Knowing William would make that very difficult.'

'I don't know why he should want two kinds of credit,' said Theresa. 'Not Richard.'

'That is beautiful of you towards him,' said Emily. 'Why shouldn't he want two kinds of credit? You wouldn't ask that if you lived with Nicholas. Living with Peter must be so ennobling. There are Lydia and Peter coming up the road. It is nice to see Peter in innocent company again. I can't meet them, Theresa. I am going home to write it all in my diary. I keep a diary, because I think I have that kind of personality. I must put in my will that it is to be destroyed at my death. For fear somebody should read it, and publish it, and pretend they had written it. Unless I leave it to Nicholas, so that he can have written a book after all. I hope he will outlive me. I would commit suicide, except that now I believe in religion, and religion does not allow that. And I am not single for the sake of Nicholas. I read in a book that no woman could love a man she did not make sacrifices for. But there is so much falseness about books. Too much, I think.'

'Emily is worth a thousand Lydias,' said Theresa, as her husband entered the study alone.

'Oh, you are too wise to talk of some people in terms of others, my dear. Emily is rare, of course.'

'Oh, you see that, do you, Peter?'

'Yes, I see that, my dear. I see.'

Theresa looked at her husband, and did not speak.

Emily went back to her brother, and found him sitting by his fire, dreamy and unoccupied.

'Well, darling,' she said. 'So you have given up your book! Have you done away with it?'

'Yes, I have destroyed it,' said Herrick, smiling at her. 'Destroyed it, my Emily. I don't like books, and that is the truth. I am quite put off them. Do you know, dear old Bumpus made a confession to Masson and me? He confessed that he had remembered his old book, called it up to his mind again, the one that was supposed to be in his friend's grave, that is actually there, and made out that it was this new one. This one he was to have read tonight. The one that was destroyed in old Crabbe's room. And to own that up before Masson and Fletcher! I couldn't have done it, Emily. And I don't think it is incumbent upon a man to keep nothing of his secret doings to himself.'

'Neither do I,' said Emily. 'We should be afraid of having anybody talk to us. And we certainly couldn't talk to anybody. I don't mean it wasn't wonderful of Dickie. But what he had done wasn't enough to be a tax on anybody. For his very worst.'

'No,' said Herrick. 'There was no great harm in it. But I confess I don't readily follow a stretch of doubleness like that. A sudden temptation and yielding to it! That I understand. I think the highest type of person might be prone to it.'

'Ever can understand that,' said Emily. 'And the lowest type of person would be even more prone to it. But everything else just follows from it. That does want a little more cleverness to understand, or else experience. But I am sure you understand it, darling. Did William and Peter say anything?'

'They neither of them said a word,' said Herrick. 'But they will not in the future. It is all over for Bumpus. Well, I don't like books, to bring old Bumpus to that. Dear old Bumpus! It was a fine thing of him, when he was a young man, and a fine thing of him now to tell us of it. He told us to tell you, Emily. He remembered your making the suggestion that he should rewrite the book. It was not easy to him, I think, to have you told. I think he found me the easiest. And I confess I like to think that.'

'So should I,' said Emily. 'You were rather unkind about me. I suppose I have proved that I should have done the same in Dickie's place. I don't know why he should find me difficult.'

'Dear old Bumpus!' said Herrick. 'My dear old gifted, erring friend! Well, well, we all err. And this kind of thing, this literary ambition, is the thing that most of all leads men to error, I think. Do you know, Emily, I think that the best achievement of a man, the highest and largest thing, is to feel tolerance and generous love for a man who can do what is denied to himself to do. I do indeed. As I feel for Bumpus tonight. As I feel for my friend. I do indeed feel it, Emily.'

'Nicholas, you really are a genius,' said Emily.

7

'Miss Basden, just come and put a stop to all this, will you? Here is Mother, getting all into a state, with nobody thought of coming! I wish this dinner party was at the bottom of the sea. Just see that she gets a breathing space, Miss Basden, will you?'

'Yes, I will, Mr Merry. I have got fairly tidy myself betimes, on purpose to prevent such naughtiness,' said Miss Basden, who wore a remote expression, for which her toilet was responsible.

'Yes, Miss Basden, how we depend on you! And what a thing, all of this! All this fuss and change, and nobody coming who can do any good to the school! All this pretending that we do not live as we do, but in different rooms, and in a different way, as if the ordinary way did not make work enough! A second rate kind of thing, I call it, for all of us to be doing. And it isn't as if Miss Herrick will not give us away, so that all of it is as good as nothing – Ah! Miss Herrick! Ah, I did not see you, Miss Herrick. We were just saying how you would give us away, you know, and talk as you will to us, so that our guests would see through all our little changes. Ah, Miss Herrick, you and I both have our way of talking, haven't we?'

'Yes, I am sure we have everything due to us. And it is so suitable for you not to like the second rate. But I am afraid the basement dining room is that. I believe Mr Bentley would think so. We ought to be going to the study, which is the drawing room tonight. We have honestly left that as it is.'

Miss Basden hurried across the hall to open the door for Emily, and Mr Merry followed as if too cast down to take this natural office upon himself.

'What a lovely family group!' said Emily, as the Fletchers came in. 'An uncle and a nephew, and a brother and a sister and an aunt, and a husband and a wife, and I think some more, all in four people! I wish Nicholas and I were something to Mr and Mrs Merry and Miss Basden.'

'Ah, you are, Miss Herrick, you are,' said Mr Merry.

'And am I to be left out? That is very lonely for me,' said Mr Burgess.

'Yes, yes, Mr Burgess,' said Mr Merry. 'Why, Mr Bentley! How are you, Mr Bentley? Why, how nice it is to have one of the fathers of our ladies here among us, like this!'

'Let us go up to the fire, Miss Bentley,' said Mrs Merry, 'and leave the men to talk about the newspapers in the cold.'

'Why, what a way for your wife to talk in your presence, Mr Merry!' said Delia.

'I don't suppose wives ought to talk at all in their husband's presence,' said Herrick.

'Civilised countries are so artificial,' said Emily. 'But you should not speak true words in jest, Nicholas. It is not open of you.'

'Well, what about us single women, Miss Herrick?' said Miss Basden.

'Well, I don't suppose we ought to talk at all. I expect we ought to be exposed at birth, or something like that.'

'How would it be known at birth which of us were going to be single?' said Delia.

'That is really clever of you,' said Emily. 'Though people exposed at birth would be single, wouldn't they?'

'Well, we were certainly classed by the state with paupers and idiots and children, before we had the vote,' said Miss Basden. 'I mean we women were.'

'And no nice children, or paupers either, and no really sensible idiots, would talk in people's presence,' said Bumpus.

'Do we go in to dinner now, and pair off like the ark?' said Emily. 'I think that is so useful. How clever of you, Nicholas, to have told everybody to take in everybody else, without telling them anything! But then men are clever.'

'Do you really think, Miss Herrick,' said Francis, as the seats were taken, 'that men are clever in such little ways, compared to ladies? I think many people would grant the ladies the palm.'

'I won't answer for my sister, Fletcher,' said Herrick. 'She will be leading you into danger. You would soon find yourself in her power.'

'I should never be anything but glad, Mr Herrick,' said Francis, leaning forward, 'to find myself in any lady's power.'

'That is rather a rash statement,' said Mr Burgess. 'I haven't lived so long as many of the people here, but I should hardly say that.'

'Ah, Mr Burgess, so you have seen life, have you?' said Mr Merry.

'I have seen life, Merry,' said Bumpus. 'Do please believe me.'

'We won't talk about that, Richard,' said Herrick.

'Nicholas is going to be a bright host!' said Emily. 'Isn't he wonderful?'

'How are your little fellows tonight, Miss Bentley?' said Mr Merry. 'They are growing, you know. We can't stop that, and we don't want to, but we have to keep an eye on them.'

'Francis, listen,' said Bumpus. 'You are the only possible future parent in this room. Bentley's boys are here.'

Mr Merry faintly sighed, as if he had indeed been working merely from habit, and Mr Bentley looked up, as though he could see no occasion for himself to speak.

'It must be so nice to have a houseful of boys,' said Miss Lydia. 'Boys and men are my province. Now, your woman is a complex creature. I don't seem to get any hold upon her. It is just meant to show us, that we are all meant for different parts of what has to be done.'

'I gather, Miss Basden, that I am not on what you would call the side of the chosen,' said Francis, with his careful laugh. 'I plead guilty to disagreeing with you on the women's suffrage question.'

'I think that these changes in the divorce laws will do a great deal towards equalising the position of women,' said Miss Basden, with terseness and rising colour.

'Miss Basden,' said Francis, after a startled pause. 'I should think any man unworthy of the name, who did not feel the old laws a crying disgrace to a civilised country, as you are brave enough to face these subjects. But I confess I should sympathise with you, if you preferred to turn your eyes from them.'

'Well, I should not sympathise with myself. I don't think that because people are safe from married dangers, they should turn their eyes from others who are not.'

'You will all have your patience tried if you go on,' said Herrick.

'But I expect they would all keep it,' said Delia, implying that this was a grave necessity.

'I do not know that, Miss Bentley,' said Francis. 'I am afraid I must confess that I yield rather easily to impatience.'

'Well, well, it is the same thing,' said Herrick. 'The one is a condensed form of the other. Patience contains more impatience than anything else, as I judge.'

'You judge well,' said Bumpus.

'How profound you are, Nicholas!' said Emily. 'I have always thought that. Though I have never known that I thought it. Think how it is with everything, how tolerance, for example, is only condensed intolerance, and how it holds more intolerance than anything else. It is just a case for intolerance to be kept in. And think how religion holds more dislike of religion than anything else!'

'Now, Uncle Peter, put them right,' said Francis.

'Well, well, I think myself,' said Mr Fletcher, 'that the old, simple views are the right ones, that patience is as far as can be from impatience, tolerance from intolerance, in a word, good from bad. I think we all think that.'

'Yes, I think we do,' said Delia, gravely.

'I do not think so,' said Emily. 'I think that good is bad condensed. I think so, because my brother has told me so. I think a woman ought to think what the men of her family think. You think that too, do you not, Francis? It is right of me to think that good is bad condensed, and holds more bad than anything else, when my brother thinks so, isn't it?'

'Ah! Miss Herrick,' said Francis, slowly shaking his head.

'Mother, you are not eating,' said Mr Merry.

'Look, what is that?' said Herrick, hurriedly, pointing to a brooch which Miss Lydia wore. 'A most curious thing! A most beautiful piece of old work! Let me see it. Be so very kind as to take it off, and pass it to me. Yes, a most exquisite thing of art, a possession for whoever owns it.'

'Oh, my brooch! Yes, I am very fond of my brooch. My dear brooch, that was given to me by a sailor man, who came back to me, so shy and awkward, dear, nice thing, to tell me that he had thought of me! Oh, I would not part with my brooch.'

'How beautiful it must be to have sailor men and brooches, and not feel that one's deathbed must be so remorseful!' said Emily.

'Ah, they are my children,' said Miss Lydia.

'You have no children, have you, Mr Fletcher?' said Delia, smiling.

'Not living,' said Mr Fletcher. 'We have had two sons.'

Theresa gazed fiercely in front of her.

'Yes, there is not much good in rearing up children, when they are to be killed off one by one.'

'It is the valuable lives that must be used,' murmured Miss Lydia. 'That is why they are so precious. Ah! How precious they were!'

Mr Fletcher looked at his women simply with solicitude. He had no thought that strangers might not have the knowledge of them, that a lifetime had given himself.

'Mrs Fletcher is very sensitive, is she not?' said Delia to Francis.

'Yes, yes, she is,' said Francis. 'She is the most sensitive creature. My uncle has had great trouble with her, to save her all that she could be saved, I mean.' Francis hastened to contradict what might be read into his words. 'It is a great responsibility to marry a good woman, and find that she is so wrought upon by things.'

'But she has been the very wife for him, I should think?' said Delia.

'Miss Bentley,' said Francis, leaning forward, 'she has been an angel to him.'

'Rather a substantial angel,' said Theresa.

'If that quality, Aunt Theresa, is not possible in angels, I am afraid that we can none of us besides Uncle Peter claim to have anything angelic about us,' said Francis.

'Well, well, if we are as well as may be, as men and women, that is enough,' said Mr Fletcher, implying that certain comparisons were not of a kind to be made.

'Uncle Peter,' said Francis, 'I thank you for your rebuke. One is so prone to get into the way of using lightly words that are to be used in a different spirit. Any check on that is very wholesome, and to me, very welcome.'

'I should not have thought that so many perfect people would be allowed to live together in one house,' said Bumpus.

'Yes, we have been allowed to live together for a long time,' said Miss Lydia, her voice dwelling on the agency. 'It has been a happy, happy time. But the end of all good things will come. We must look for it. It is that, that makes them so good. But we shall go on being happy. We have all so much work to do.'

'We shall go on being happy, too,' said Miss Basden. 'We have plenty of work to do here as well.'

'Yes, you have, Miss Basden,' said Mr Merry.

'Miss Basden, it is a thing not to be so thankful for,' said Francis, his tone correcting possible regret and shame in Miss Basden, in earning her bread.

'Yes, yes, of course,' said Herrick. 'We all feel that in this house, I am sure. Why, I work from early morning to late at night. And I never take a holiday. I can't see what people want with holidays myself.'

'What do you say to that, Mr Burgess?' said Mr Merry.

'Well, I was expecting that, Mr Merry. We have discussed that question, and understand each other now on it, I think.'

Mr Burgess opened the door for the women.

'Mr Burgess is a beautiful advertisement,' said Emily, as they reached the study. 'He shows almost an arrogance. Fancy having that for boys!'

'He has his points,' said Miss Basden.

'You are a martyr, Miss Basden,' said Emily. 'The worst of a beautiful advertisement is, that it does need that.'

'Let us talk quickly about servants,' said Mrs Merry, smiling, 'before the men come in.'

'It must be so dreadful to be a servant,' said Emily, 'and do the important work of the world. That sort of work, so ill paid and degrading.'

'Well, well, it depends upon others. And women vary so, vary so,' said Miss Lydia.

'Well, I do not really think it would be such a bad life,' said Delia. 'If I belonged to the working class, I would rather be a servant than many other things.'

'And yet you don't think it is a bad life', said Emily, 'putting it like that! Fancy having to be of nice appearance, and quick and willing and trustworthy, and not wear spectacles waiting at table, as if one's sight would alter then!' Emily put up her glass. 'It must be very bad to be all that, or anything except the first.

And I have never met people of that quality, except Peter and William. And they are neither of them quick. And I am not sure of Peter's appearance.'

Theresa laughed.

'Well now, Mr Herrick, we have all been remiss in not asking you when your book is coming out,' said Francis, as the men came in. 'A novel? Is that what they call it? But when is your book coming out, if I may put it in a safe way?'

'Oh, well, I believe very likely not at all. Perhaps I have come to your implied view of it,' said Herrick.

'Oh, well, I shouldn't perhaps have put it in the way I did. And what does my view have to do with it? But I will confess that it did strike me as not a quite expected thing, that you should give your time to writing a book, that any lady might have written. I don't mean that a lady could write your book. You won't take me to mean what I don't mean?'

'Mr Fletcher, you are not blind, surely, to the fact that women often equal and surpass men in literary achievements?' said Miss Basden.

'Well, Miss Basden, I plead guilty to being old-fashioned in these matters. It is my inclination to put women on a plane of their own, and to regard them as coming down from it, when they take upon themselves the things that have been held fitter for men. And that perhaps leads to my implying that they do not do so well in those things. But I was meaning quite the opposite of disrespect to them, I assure you.'

'Oh, I see. There is the usual kind of contempt in that sentimental exaltation of women.'

'Miss Basden, believe me, it never has been so with me,' said Francis, earnestly.

'If Francis should marry Miss Basden,' said Emily to Theresa, 'the school would go down just as Nicholas begins to need the comforts of old age. Unless he would live here with her.'

'He is good at living in other people's houses,' said Theresa.

'I suppose living with him would embitter one,' said Emily.

'Suppose Merry should be embittered!' said Bumpus. 'His personality would go to pieces.'

'Miss Basden apologises for being a spinster rather more often than is necessary,' said Emily. 'Of course I don't mean it is not necessary, up to a point.'

'And his marrying her would put a stop to her being self-supporting,' said Bumpus. 'That is what he does not like about her.'

'Where is my wife?' said Mr Merry.

'She has run away and deserted us,' said Delia.

'She has gone up to sit for a few minutes in her room, I think, Mr Merry,' said Miss Basden, stooping over the fire.

'Is she not well?' said Herrick, loudly. 'Allow me, allow me, Miss Basden.

'Yes, I think so, Mr Herrick,' said Miss Basden. 'She just wanted a few minutes to herself, as she does sometimes.'

'Not when she has guests!' said Herrick, still rather loudly.

'Hers is a solitary nature, I suppose,' said Miss Lydia, looking up.

'I think we owe this coffee to her,' said Masson, as a tray was brought in followed by Mrs Merry.

'William, what a charming first word of the evening for you to speak!' said Bumpus. 'Giving someone her due.'

'We are very grateful to her for it,' said Miss Basden. 'Coffee is a thing I never take on myself. I plead guilty to managing it much less well than Mrs Merry.'

'I should like there to be no such thing as food, myself,' said Mrs Merry, leaning back in her chair.

'Yes, Mother,' said Mr Merry.

Francis looked at Mrs Merry with long and almost inquiring sympathy.

'We must not ask our friends to dinner again, must we, Merry?' said Mr Herrick in a low tone, breathing deeply.

'Oh, Mr Herrick!' said Mr Merry, leaning towards him. 'Oh, you are not right, you know. Not if you take us up seriously, just when we are just feeling a little for you, in this little disturbance. No, no, not a disturbance, a pleasure for us all. Yes, yes, we all know.'

'I never can remember to eat, myself,' said Miss Basden, in a tone that addressed the company. 'If I can remember, I always do, because I think one can do so much more, if one eats.'

'Ah, Miss Basden,' said Mr Merry, his voice somehow dying away.

'Ah, the pleasures of our bodies!' said Miss Lydia, with the last word lower. 'They are given to us as things that are right for us. If they are used rightly. If they are used rightly.'

'Charles, have you finished your coffee, dear?' said Mrs Merry.

'Charles?' said Masson. 'Oh, it is Merry's Christian name.'

'How simple and kindly of him it seems to have one!' said Emily.

'A king's name, too,' said Bumpus.

'Mrs Merry, have you a name, apart from the maternal one by which we hear you designated?' said Mr Burgess.

Mr Merry's eyes went to Mr Burgess.

'Yes, my name is Emily,' said Mrs Merry.

'My third name is Emily,' said Miss Basden. 'What a lot of namesakes we are!'

'Yes, Miss Basden, very nice,' said Mr Merry, his voice just avoiding a note of depreciation.

'And, Miss Basden, if I may ask, what are your other two names?' said Francis.

Miss Basden repeated two names, and there was a faint titter from one of the maids who were removing the coffee table.

'Mother,' said Mr Merry, throwing a fierce glance from habit towards the titter, and rapidly withdrawing it, 'what is it you were saying?'

'I hope Mrs Merry will be quick, before Miss Basden has a fourth name,' said Bumpus. 'Francis' mind is working towards it. She did not say she stopped at three.'

'Oh, didn't she imply it?' said Emily. 'The kitchen maid, who is second parlour maid tonight, must find it too much.'

'Isn't it too much?' said Theresa.

'How good we all are at talking without ever saying anything we think!' said Bumpus.

'It is not always politic to say what we think,' said Miss Basden.

'It is not so easy,' said Masson.

'Sometimes I suppose it is right to say it, whether or not we like it, and whether or not it is liked,' said Delia.

'Yes, yes, the thing to be done,' said Miss Lydia, sighing.

'Oh, just possibly. Once or twice in a lifetime,' said Mr Bentley to his daughter.

'Nearer once than twice,' said Bumpus.

'Oh, everyone is not a man,' said Theresa.

'No, that would be a queer state of things,' said Miss Basden.

'Yes,' said Bumpus. 'Suppose there had to be two under-masters instead of you and Burgess!'

'Oh, Mr Bumpus!' said Miss Basden.

'Well, would two undermistresses do instead of the two of us?' said Mr Burgess, not feeling self-suppression a duty in this case. 'Or is prejudice the one thing regarded in this school?'

'No, no, Mr Burgess. Come, you know it is not,' said Mr Merry. 'You are the only sop to it. I mean… what I meant was, Mr Burgess, that if it didn't matter about having a man on the staff, we should still have been glad to have you, you know. That is what I meant, Mr Burgess.'

'I meant that, too,' said Bumpus.

'Oh, well, Mr Merry, you are very kind. But it doesn't sound as if you would have been much good to me, much compensation to me, in the event of my not being a man.'

Mr Burgess noted Miss Basden's expression, and relapsed into peace.

'I should think you are all great readers, Fletcher,' said Herrick. 'Miss Fletcher, now, are you not a great person for books?'

'Oh, my books! Yes, I am very fond of my books,' said Miss Lydia. 'My dear books, that live in my special case! I love them very much. I am always excited when I have a new companion for them. Yes, I am a great person for my books.'

'Have you a particular kind?' said Herrick.

'Yes,' said Miss Lydia, raising her eyes without lifting her head. 'History! Nearly all my books are historical, or if not, biographical. I should think I have no read a novel for thirty years.'

'What books do you read most, Mr Fletcher?' said Delia, to Francis.

'Miss Bentley, the book I read the most, is, I am thankful to say, the Old Book. My life is largely made up of what must be called the sordid things of the world. But I have the one great privilege.'

'Yes, yes, we can all do with that book. A very good book!' said Herrick.

'Miss Basden, what do you read?' said Emily. 'Only the Bible or not?'

'Well, I read a good deal of French, Miss Herrick. I do not know how it is, but I always enjoy books so much more, when they are in French. I feel so much more at home in the language, somehow. Now I very seldom read an English book.'

'How wonderful and educational for the boys of you! But what kind of books do you read?'

'Oh, all kinds. I really do not mind, as long as they are French. Or if not French, Italian or German. What I do not like to read, is an English book.'

'Well, Miss Basden, we can very few of us say that,' said Francis.

'I believe I really read the Bible the most, too,' said Delia.

'It is a good thing we did not all live in the time when the Bibles were chained up in the churches,' said Bumpus. 'It would have been so lonely.'

'Well, but it is a good thing to read the Bible,' said Francis.

'Of course it is the most beautiful book,' said Emily. 'And now we are modern, and only read about wickedness, it is so nice to have it unchained, isn't it? It really ought to be chained, I think.'

'Ah, you try to get at us, Miss Herrick,' said Francis, not quite checking a laugh.

'Ah, there is much warning in it for us,' said Miss Lydia.

'In all great pictures,' said Francis, firmly pulling himself together, and finding the effort inspiring, 'we are shown the dreadful as well as the beautiful. We are surely not given only one side of the lesson.'

'I am one of the greatest readers alive,' said Herrick. 'I have read all European modern literature, the enormous bulk of it. And I have read as much medieval literature as any man living. And I know my Greek and Latin. They were taught to us well when I was a boy.'

'But you need not imply how they are taught now,' said Bumpus.

'What do you read, Mr Masson?' said Mrs Merry.

'Very little off my own line, Mrs Merry. Miss Austen is the novelist I read the most.'

'What do you think of her books, Mr Fletcher?' said Delia to Francis.

'I am afraid, Miss Bentley, that I have very little use for books written by ladies for ladies, if I may so express myself, though I dare say I should be the better for them.'

'Oh, no, you would not. You could not be,' said Bumpus.

'It is the other way round,' said Masson.

'Personally, I can't get over the littleness in her books,' said Miss Basden.

'Ah, we are not small enough, not small enough,' said Miss Lydia.

'The best goods are done up in a certain way,' said Mr Fletcher, smiling.

'It is my great regret that Jane Austen died so young,' said Masson.

'And one used to think that forty was not so young after all,' said Herrick.

'I never think about my age,' said Miss Basden.

'Ah, but we are in progress,' breathed Miss Lydia, 'simply in progress.'

'To what may be big enough in the end for us,' said Theresa.

'One is really a hero for not committing suicide, I suppose,' said Mr Burgess.

'Now, Mr Burgess, none of that sort of talk with the boys,' said Mr Merry.

'Oh, I very seldom talk to the boys, Mr Merry.'

'I hope no one has seen me talking to my undergraduates,' said Bumpus.

'No one has. Don't boast, Dickie,' said Emily.

'We must be going,' said Theresa.

'So must we,' said Delia. 'We ought to be quite ashamed of staying so long, oughtn't we, Father?'

'It has been too great a pleasure for us to feel compunction about seeming to appreciate it,' said Mr Bentley, his voice falling with an unfamiliar sound.

'Thank you for coming and bearing it all,' said Emily. 'It has been a great thing for us to have such glimpses of family life. My brother and I are orphans, you know.'

'And I am half an orphan,' said Mr Burgess. 'So it is very suitable all round.'

'Now, look here, Mr Burgess,' said Mr Merry, in a low tone, 'there is no need for you to be standing about, saying goodbye to everyone, you know. Now suppose you go off somewhere to have a smoke, you know.'

'Goodbye, Mr Fletcher.' Mr Merry took upon himself the duties of host. 'No more prizes yet for you to give away. The lads like to work for their rewards, bless them. And Mr Bentley. Ah, the two boys! I won't tell you now what we think of them, because that must be kept for a day when we have had less pleasure.'

Mr Merry returned to the sitting room, rubbing his hands, and looking about him with much fondness, as if using up the residue of the feelings gathered for his guests.

'Well, we shall start off work tomorrow with quite a spurt,' said Miss Basden.

'Yes, Miss Basden,' said Mr Merry. 'Not that you are in much need of that.'

'Well, but it is an opportunity for you to get a hit at me, Mr Merry,' said Mr Burgess, strolling back into the room.

'Oh, Mr Burgess! Get a hit at you! Why, you try to misunderstand me, unless you like to be treated as if you were seventy. Good night, Miss Herrick. And Mr Herrick. Yes, Mr Burgess. Are you coming up with us? Such a pleasure to us all. Not at all a trouble. I mean, what a pleasure in proportion to the little arranging, you know.'

Mr Merry hastened after his wife, as if fearing to break his impression.

'Well, I have not much to boast of,' said Herrick, sitting down by the fire. 'Seventy years old, and nothing before me, and nothing behind to count! Why, I could almost envy Merry, for being only fifty, and wanting nothing more than he has.'

'You should not talk about "almost envying" Mr Merry, as if he belonged to people like that,' said Emily. 'And I don't know about his not wanting more than he has. I don't think he wants that much. And fifty isn't such a good age as all that. And not much to boast of! With seventy years of safe life behind you, when most people have the risk of having so much less! And all the life in front of you, that people of seventy always have!'

'Yes, yes, Emily. I dare say I shall have a time yet. Time to do something in. It sometimes happens that the end of a man's life sums him up. There is no great wrong about being an exception. Exceptions are more worthy of interest in a way. I don't think I have ever been quite on the ordinary line.'

'No, I am sure you have not. It would have been dreadful of you.'

Biographical note

Dame Ivy Compton-Burnett was born in Pinner on 5th June 1884; the daughter of an illustrious homeopathic doctor, James Compton-Burnett, she was one of twelve children by two marriages. The family moved to Hove in 1891, due to her father's belief in the medicinal benefits of sea air.

Following her father's death when she was seventeen, Compton-Burnett studied Classics at Royal Holloway College in Surrey. Her mother's death in 1911 left Compton-Burnett a trustee of her four youngest siblings' inheritance and she took on the role of the head of house, keen to keep the family together. However, her family life was to be marked by tragedy with four out of five of her full siblings dying young. One brother, Guy, died of pneumonia, the other, Noel, was killed at the Somme and her two youngest sisters died in a suicide pact on Christmas day. None of the twelve children had children of their own. Compton-Burnett herself contracted influenza in 1918 and, having been found unconscious, was dangerously ill for a month.

Compton-Burnett spent much of her life as companion to Margaret Jourdain, the antiquarian furniture expert, living in a flat in Kensington with her from 1919. Her first novel, *Dolores* was published in 1911; it was however, *Pastors and Masters*, written in 1925, that was to prove the beginning of her career as a novelist. The main themes of her work generally revolved around the undercurrents of emotions that were concealed beneath the calm surface of Victorian households and society. She was also particularly praised for her ability to recreate everyday scenes from 'below stairs'. In the years that followed, Compton-Burnett wrote a novel almost every other year and surrounded herself with a literary circle of friends.

Compton-Burnett was awarded a DBE in 1967 and elected as a Companion of the Royal Society of Literature. She died in 1969 having written twenty novels during her lifetime.